TO DIE IN TOLEDO

by Robert Rahula

ALSO BY ROBERT RAHULA

NOVELS:
Messieurs
Panamaniac
Island of Misfits
Day Another Paradise In
One Last Fling
Bathhouse Stories
Conversation in a Belgian Bar
All the Yage in Reno
Exigent Circumstances
Uninvited Guest
A Modest Summation of Things

SHORT STORIES:
Horror Stories for Children

POETRY:
Trigger Points
Dentro Del Corazón Bloqueada
Camino
Migration
I Sing the Body Politic
Wonderland
From Whose Bourn
Poemas Españoles
Expat Poems

ANTHOLOGIES:
Half Life
The Essential Dan Landes
50 Years Down the Drain

TO DIE IN TOLEDO

www.robertrahula.com

This is a work of fiction. Characters, organizations, businesses, products, locales, and events portrayed in this book either are products of the author's imagination or are used fictitiously.

ISBN 978-1-7329708-6-1

Alma-gator Press

Barcelona · Madrid · La Chorrera

"There are an infinite number of universes
and each one of those infinite universes
contain an infinite number of realities."

-Stephen Hawking

CHAPTER ONE

So, I went to Europe... and I died.

I'm not quite sure when it actually happened, but obviously it was in Toledo, Spain. That's where I got sick. I remember not being able to walk more than ten steps without getting dizzy and out of breath. I didn't want to look like a feeble old tourist, so I would stop and pretend to consult a map on my cell phone, or pretend to gaze into a shop window, until I could catch my breath. But my whole body ached. I felt weak and stupid. I had no idea what was wrong. At first, I thought it was just the steep hills of Toledo, but after a few days I realized that something was wrong with me. The shortness of breath simply would not go away. I started worrying that it was my heart, so I searched for a cardiologist on Google Maps. There was only one name that popped up, but no telephone number, so I took a taxi over to his loca tion. His office was closed, but luckily for me he was there doing some paperwork. He reluctantly let me in, and after I explained my situation, he gave me an EKG. He told me my heart was in fibrillation and that I needed to get to a hospital right away. He wrote something in Spanish on a piece of paper, stapled it to the EKG printout, gave me the name of the nearest hospital, and told me to take a cab there. I thanked him, paid him, and followed his advice.

I remember the hospital. They read the doctor's note and admitted me right away—no waiting. They put me in a bed, hooked me up to another EKG, and stuck a drip feed into my arm. They told me it contained medicine. Over the next twenty-four hours, I was moved from room to room. Different doctors came in, looked at the EKG monitor, and talked to me. I remember various noises and people moving all around me. I must have been delirious because it's all a blur to me now.

I figure I must have died that night.

The thing that they don't tell you about death is that you just continue. You don't disappear. You don't go to heaven or hell. There's no long tunnel, no pearly white gates, no judgment, no purgatory, no revelation, no enlightenment... you just continue with your "life" as if it were a dream. You don't even realize you have died. You feel like you're in your body; events and images continue to occur before your eyes; you feel sensation; you can think; it all feels like the life you've always known... except you are dead.

Let me explain... or at least, let me explain what I think it's all about. There is a real life, and we are born into it. And we accumulate all these memories and images and experiences... and then we die, but our consciousness continues, and it works the same way our brains work when we sleep, and we continue to draw on our memories and images and experiences in order to dream. That's all life is when you're dead: a dream. Maybe that's all life is when you're alive, I don't know. But I do know that when you're dead, you continue to experience life just like when you were alive... except... except that there are no new experiences. When you're dead, you can't experience anything you've never experienced before—you can only re-experience things you've already lived through. It's like dreaming, where your subconscious rehashes all the different experiences you've ever had, combines them with your current worries, and throws them up like images on a screen in front of your dreaming eyes. But the difference between life and death is that after you die you simply cannot experience anything that is totally new. You can imagine it, but you can't experience it. For example, if you never skydived when you were alive, you can't skydive after you die. You can imagine it, but you can't do it. That's how you know you're dead—there are no more brand-new experiences. You can only rehash and recombine old experiences. Being dead is like being locked in a library with all the DVDs you've already watched. All you can do is watch them again. There are no new DVDs arriving.

So anyway, I spent the night at the hospital in Toledo. The next morning, a doctor came in and talked to me. She told me I should probably cut my European vacation short and return home to see my regular cardiologist. She wrote out several prescriptions for me, and then they discharged me. I took a cab back to my hotel and booked a flight home.

I thought about returning to the States, but I have lived in Panama for so many years that it has become my home. Besides, my cardiologist is there. So I booked a flight back to Panama City, and had a friend pick me up at the airport to take me home to Villa Rosario. Oddly enough, I don't remember the flight at all. Somehow, suddenly, I was home.

Over the next few weeks, I saw my cardiologist and had more tests. He tweaked my medications a few times, told me to take it easy and let time do its work. Gradually, as I eased back into my normal routine, I began to feel better.

I don't know when it first began to dawn on me that I was dead. I think my first clue was that "lack of new experience" thing that I mentioned. There is a stale quality to life when you're dead. Nothing gets you excited like it used to. There's nothing to look forward to. I began to notice that every day was more or less the same. I began yearning for some new experience, a new taste in food, a new relationship, new thoughts, anything new... but nothing happened.

So anyway, that's the first thing to understand about being dead: nothing changes. Nothing ends. You just go on repeating and rehashing everything that's ever happened before.

As an aside, I would say to those people whose lives are so wretched that they are contemplating suicide: *don't* do it. It won't change anything. You're better off trying to change your life situation for the better. Trust me on this. Stay alive and do whatever it takes to make your life better. Try and live as long as you can. You will thank me later after you finally die.

Also, as a hint to those who are unsure whether they're dead or alive—try to do something completely new, something you've never done before. If you can't do it, you're dead.

CHAPTER TWO

So, anyway, to begin with, let me describe what my life is like, as a dead person. As I said before, life appears normal. These phantoms around me... well, they appear alive. They move and talk like real people, and I talk with them as if I were still alive. Each moment seems real enough. Other than nothing new happening, it's not that horrible being dead.

I live in Villa Rosario, a small town in Panama. (It would be more accurate to say "I *used* to live in Villa Rosario," but I don't want to keep repeating the imperfect tense in all my sentences, and so, since I experience life as a continuation of present moments, I will just use the present tense.) I live in Villa Rosario, in a small apartment in a medium-sized apartment building. It's a quiet building, full of old expat gringo pensioners like me. All of them, like me, are long-term residents of this building... except one. One of the residents is a newbie, a younger retiree named Herald, who is just trying out the expatriate lifestyle for the first time. He won't make it. We all know that. He's from Oklahoma. He's got the wrong personality to be a self-reliant expat living in a foreign country. Oklahomans don't make for good expats. You can't be full of shit and make it as an expat. The cultural differences will chew you up and spit you out. The other tenants and I have a money wager on how long he'll last. I bet twenty dollars he'll be gone in six weeks.

The problem with most expats, especially norteamericano expats, and especially norteamericano expats from Oklahoma, is that they talk too much. They feel like they don't exist unless they are spouting their opinions to someone else. They claim they are just "being friendly," but what they are really doing is justifying their own existence. Herald fits that bill.

For example, if I'm out on my little second floor balcony in the morning enjoying a cup of coffee and watching the blue sky, and he happens to step out from his first-floor apartment and looks up and sees me, he can't help but launch into a soliloquy:

"Good morning Robert! Isn't it a beautiful day? I was just thinking to myself this morning how smart I was to move down here where every day is so beautiful. Just gorgeous. What a great day! How's the world treating you? I checked the weather in Oklahoma this morning and it's seventeen degrees. Seventeen degrees! I bet my friends are all freezing their asses off! Ha. I'm so glad I'm here."

And he does it all in one breath.

It's hard to know where to start in deconstructing his verbal diarrhea. Obviously, it's a beautiful day. I wouldn't be out on my balcony trying to enjoy the day if it wasn't beautiful. So, I don't need him to point out the obvious to me. And he's not actually trying to share anything with me. He's just trying to get me to agree with him, to give him confirmation, so that he knows his existence—his perception of the day— is real. Notice how he asks how I'm doing but doesn't wait for a response. That's because he's not interested in how I'm doing. Then he goes on to reaffirm that he's from Oklahoma and that he left Oklahoma and now he's living down here in a place that is different than Oklahoma... again, he's just trying to confirm that his existence is real.

But I know that his existence is not real. It's not real because he's not real. He's just an amalgam of people I've met from Oklahoma. He's just someone I've created. He's just a fantasy that I'm conjuring up out of all my experiences and memories of all the yokels, blowhards, idiots, and dumbass blabbermouth ranch hands and car salesmen that I've ever met. I don't know why I created him, but I did. That's what you do when you're dead—you create these people out of old memories to populate your dream of life. You recycle your memories. That's all dreams are... and when you're dead, all you do is dream of life.

But I don't mean to be too negative about it. I'm just trying to explain how it is. The fact is, it *is* a beautiful day. And I was enjoying it until he came outside. So I wave and get up and come inside to refill my coffee cup and give him time to go away.

The fact is, all the gringos who live in this building are a little crazy, some crazier than others. You have to be a little crazy to want to be an expat, to leave your own country and culture to try to make a new life in another country. If you weren't crazy when you left the States, the life of being an expat will make you crazy.

Joey is probably our craziest expat gringo, but he's lived here so long that we're all used to him. Most of the time we don't even notice how totally off his rocker he is. He's always wrapped up in some conspiracy theory. He's probably clinically paranoid but, like I say, we're all used to him. If you're used to something, no matter how bizarre it is, you accept it as normal.

For example, whenever two or three of us expats are sitting talking together, he will approach us with the latest revelation of how "they" are fucking with us.

"See, I told you that that Kim Jong Un was behind the coronavirus attack. Remember how he promised to send Trump a 'Christmas gift?' Look at this article here. See this chart that shows that North Korea didn't have any corona cases? That's because they inoculated their people before seeding China with the disease. This professor at Stanford University lays it all out. I told you North Korea was behind this!"

We all just let him talk until he's out of steam, and then we turn the discussion back to whatever we were talking about before, and he wanders away. He's crazy, but relatively harmless.

That's one of the skills you need to survive as an expat in another country: you have to have a healthy tolerance for other crazy expats, because they're all nuts, especially the gringos. Gringo expats always end up nuts, because they start off nuts. They always start with the premise that they are unhappy where they are, but that there is some "paradise" somewhere else, somewhere "free" and "life-sustaining" where they can "be themselves" or "find themselves" or "lose themselves" or whatever bullshit rationale they use. But the fact is, there is no paradise, and whatever place they left back in the States was just as good and just as fucked up as any so-called paradise they find.

But in any country, refugees (which is what we expats are) tend to gather together, because despite all of our self-proclaimed independence, we need each other, and so we learn to ignore the obvious signs of mental illness in each other. We need someone to sit with once or twice a day, just so we can hear English being spoken. Hearing English somehow grounds us, reassures us, makes us feel just a tiny bit normal for a few minutes. Everyone feels better when they hear their mother tongue. That's why it's called a "mother tongue." The sound wraps itself around you like a warm blanket during feeding time, and then every understanding becomes instinctual without having to go through the process of thinking.

CHAPTER THREE

Speaking of English, most gringos don't realize what it is about English that makes it so comforting to hear. They think it's the sound, or the fluidity, or the ability to express beautiful thoughts... but that's not it. I mean, those are comforting aspects of any language, but what makes English so particularly comforting for gringos to hear is that it has these rigid rules, and those rules impose a fixed order on the world. Gringos never realize those rules; they are not taught them in school; rather, they are hardwired into our gringo brains. And those rules have to do with the order in which words are expressed. And that order is as follows:

1. opinion
2. size
3. age
4. shape
5. color
6. origin
7. material
8. purpose
9. noun

You can leave any number of the words out, but you cannot change the order, or the sentence will just not sound right.

Take, for example, the phrase "a beautiful large old oval white New England porcelain serving dish." It contains many more adjectives than you would normally use, but if you say it out loud, it doesn't sound wrong. You understand the meaning. But if you were to mix up those adjectives and say "a New England oval white beautiful large serving porcelain old dish" it would make no sense and sound jarring to the ear. You notice this any time there's more than one adjective. You can say "big yellow taxi," and it sounds normal, but if you say "yellow big taxi," it just sounds wrong. English is completely rigid about these rules, and we never realize it. But it's the repetition of those rules that gives order to our brains. The comfort comes from familiarity, but the familiarity comes, not from the *sound* of the words, but from the *order* of the words. English is all about imposing order on a wild and unpredictable world. And gringos love order. They are blindly attracted to any kind of system, any kind of order... they have no tolerance for ambiguity. They don't want to think for themselves. Just like the rigid order of words is hardwired into the language center of our brains without us even being aware of it, gringos' need for some authority to tell them what to believe and what to do is hardwired into our culture without us having any consciousness of it. Gringos are the epitome of true believers, despite their protests that they are free and independent thinkers.

But I digress. I was talking about my life—I guess I should call it my afterlife—in Villa Rosario. I retired here more than a decade ago... well, more than a decade before I died anyway... and I live a pretty simple life here. I survive on my Social Security and a little bit of money I make writing a vlog for the *Solipsistic Times*, which is an online video-journal for wannabe nomads back in the States. I gather that most of the subscribers are van-lifers, ex-hippies, preppers, spiritual wanderers, and general misfits—my kind of people. My vlog is called "Be of the Moment, not from the Moment." I really have no idea what that means, but the owners of the channel approached me a few years back and asked me to write a script for a short weekly video under that title. I wasn't interested until they mentioned they would pay me. Nothing changes a gringo's mind more than money, and I'm no exception. It's not a lot of money, but it's steady, so every week I crank out some bullshit about staying positive in difficult times, or ten ways to energize your routine, or some sort of pseudo-new-age bullshit. I actually feel like quite the hypocrite for some of the things I write, but then the direct-deposit check arrives in my bank account, and I feel better. Now, understand, I don't read or perform the vlog—I just write it. They have some actor read it... or maybe it's a computerized voice, I don't know... but somebody else reads it, and that voice is superimposed over peaceful images of beaches or mountains or some other crap. I try not to watch it because it's such bullshit, but the owners seem happy, and as long as they continue to pay me, I'll continue to write the column.

Last week, for example, I wrote a piece on "Using Your Exercise Class to Reprogram Your Mind" where I talked about how to think about every push-up pushing destructive thoughts and judgments out of your mind; and how to use every sit-up to think about sitting up and noticing all the beauty around you. Pretty nauseating, eh? But they're not that hard to write. I just try to imagine I'm a thirteen-year-old girl who's all positive and who loves Cosmo, and the scripts just seem to write themselves. Occasionally the owners will send me ideas for future scripts, usually because they've got some sponsor lined up and they want to plug their product. The other day, they asked me to write something along the lines of "Buddhist Detachment and Quercetin Supplements." That's going to be a bit of a challenge. I'll probably write something about meditation and the simple life, then work into the topic of eating wholesome foods, and then mention nutritional supplements.

I usually spend a day or two each week working on those scripts, and then the rest of my week is free. During the day I walk around town and just observe things. I confess, I drink a certain amount, so that occupies my evenings. I've noticed that almost all the expats here either have, or have had, a drinking problem (although some of them don't think it's a problem). It must come with the territory. Everyone in the building is either an alcoholic or a reformed alcoholic. In fact, I'm not sure I could trust someone who doesn't drink or didn't used to drink. Two of the residents of this apartment building are ex-alcoholics. Some of their stories are pretty wild—no wonder they had to stop drinking. Me, I'm a quiet drunk. I like to drink alone and then slip off to bed. I don't have a lot of wild drinking stories, mostly because I don't like people, and so I avoid them. Wild drinking stories, by definition, need other people.

CHAPTER FOUR

So, as I mentioned, I first began to suspect I was dead when I realized that my "life" (as a dead person) seemed rather stale... that there weren't any new experiences. And the more I thought about this, the more it began to bug me that I hadn't done more when I was alive. And I began to wonder why it was I had been so careful, so circumspect with my life.

I suppose it was because I had this knack for always being able to see the outcome of any particular move, any particular life choice. I blame that on learning how to play Go at an early age. For those of you not familiar with Go, it is one of the oldest board games in the world, originating in China sometime before 2000 B.C. Like most board games, it is a game of war where two players fight over who can conquer the most territory. And like chess, the ability to play well involves learning how to anticipate the outcome of any particular move on the gameboard.

I learned to play as a child and played all through high school and college. I still own a beautiful wooden Go board that I bought at Madam Toguri's in Chicago. Iva Ikuko Toguri was the owner of that store. She was a Japanese-American born in Los Angeles in 1916. She made the mistake of visiting Japan in July, 1941, to care for an ailing relative, and was trapped there after the attack on Pearl Harbor. She was arrested by the Japanese authorities. They tried to pressure her to renounce her US citizenship, but she refused. She was subsequently coerced into participating in radio broadcasts where her role was limited to introducing music. After the war, she was investigated by the Armed Services who determined that she had not engaged in any propaganda activities or any criminal acts. However, when she tried to return to the US, she encountered fierce anti-Japanese hysteria, and was singled out by anti-communist gossip columnist Walter Winchell. She became maligned and mocked as "Tokyo Rose," and was subsequently arrested and charged with eight counts of treason. She was convicted of one count of treason, and served six years of a ten-year sentence. She was released in 1956 and moved to Chicago where she opened Madam Toguri's, a small shop that sold furniture, fabrics, gifts, and Go boards. In 1976, an investigation by the Chicago Tribune revealed that her indictment had been obtained via perjured testimony, and that the FBI had also coached witnesses to give false testimony against her at trial. Further investigation proved the truth of what the Armed Forces had originally determined—that she had been coerced into working for the radio broadcasts, but was never involved in any propaganda or criminal act. In 1977, President Gerald Ford gave her a full and unconditional pardon and restored her citizenship. In 2006, the American Veterans Center awarded her the Edward J. Herlihy Citizen Award, stating that she was a "patriotic American woman who was wrongfully dubbed the infamous Tokyo Rose."

These details are not germane to my point about how I learned to see the outcome of moves, but I tell you these details for two reasons: first, to point out that some people's lives are much harder than yours or mine, and yet they manage to persevere; and second, to explain why I value my Go board so much. Not only does it remind me of Iva Toguri, but it's also a beautiful piece of art, as a Go board should be. The board itself is a heavy piece of wood, almost four inches thick. And with its four intricately carved wooden legs, it sits about eight inches off the floor, or whatever table or playing surface you put it on. There are two dark wooden bowls, one which holds white shell stones for one player, and the other which holds black shale stones for the other player. None of those cheap plastic stones that portable Go sets use—these are true carved shale and shell stones that the players use to make their moves on the surface of the Go board.

But back to my point, which was metaphorical. I could have said that I learned to play chess as a child and came to view life as one big chess game. But the truth is that I learned to play Go, although the metaphor is the same: that I came to view life as a series of either good or bad moves; and that by playing Go, I learned at an early age to anticipate the outcomes of various moves on the gameboard. And I believe that somehow this skill transferred into my life—that I wanted to foresee the outcomes of personal choices, and so I learned to always analyze any personal choice in terms of the range of foreseeable outcomes. And as anyone who has played such games can tell you, the winning comes more from not making a bad move than in making a good move. So, I came to believe that success in life lay in dodging bullets, in avoiding traps. And I got pretty good at it. At least, I *thought* I was pretty good at it... up until I died anyway. In retrospect, I think I was only good at predicting when other people were making a bad move with their lives. This, of course, is not an uncommon skill. Almost everyone has it, or thinks they have it—an ability to determine when *someone else* is fucking up their life. It's a skill I still use every day. Take Herald, for instance. He speaks no Spanish, yet he wants to "live the expat life" here in Panama without learning Spanish. The first day I met him, just after he moved into this building, I tried to give him the name of a small school here in Villa Rosario that offers Spanish classes for gringos, but he told me he didn't need to learn Spanish. He said, and I quote, *"My American dollars speak enough Spanish for me."* And it is true that dollars are accepted down here as well as Panamanian balboas. And it's also true that the bartenders, hotel staff, restaurant staff, hookers, and madams at the brothels all speak English. And since that's as far as Herald's world extends, he'll get by just fine with his Oklahoma English. But he'll never understand what the waiters are saying when they mock him in Spanish behind his back. He'll never meet the real people of Panama. He'll never get beyond his world of restaurants, bars, and brothels. He's not an expat—he's just another rich white North American asswipe who wants to be on a permanent vacation, drink pina coladas at the beach, and fuck a different whore every night. The world is full of such people.

Anyway, the fact that he expressed such a disdain of any need to learn Spanish on the first day that I met him was just more evidence in my assessment that he wouldn't last more than six weeks down here. That, plus his loud offensive manner and a constant need for validation disguised as bragging, all told me that he didn't have the "right stuff" to make it here long-term. The fact is, you can't be a true expatriate anywhere in the world if you don't try to learn the language.

So, the day after I met Herald, I placed my bet with a few of the other residents of this building: Tom, Ralph, Dave, and Emile. Over the years, the five of us have created this game of each betting twenty dollars on any new tenant, on how long they'll stay in Panama. The maximum time you can bet on is one year. Winner takes the pot. If someone stays more than a year, then there is no winner, and we use the hundred dollars to take that person out for dinner.

But I have digressed again. My point was that it was fairly easy for me to predict how long Herald would last. Over the ten years or so that I've lived here, I've seen innumerable expat-wannabees come and go, and they all fit a certain pattern. First of all, they are very sure of themselves. Secondly, they are very full of themselves. Thirdly, they have no sense of wonder. And fourthly, they are not grateful. Gratitude brings a certain humility, a realization that you have received blessings that you were not entitled to, and yet you were given them anyway. You can't feel entitled *and* be grateful at the same time—it just doesn't work that way. Approximately eighty percent of gringos who move down here claiming they are going to be expatriates end up moving back to the States within two years—it's a statistical fact. I can't speak to all eighty percent. I can only say that one hundred percent of the ones I have met who went back were self-entitled, opinionated, arrogant, ungrateful, privileged assholes. Just sayin'.

But I have wandered very far from my original point, which was that when it dawned on me that I was dead, I began to realize that I had not lived life as fully as I might have, that I had spent too much time analyzing the outcomes of various "moves" of life with the intention of avoiding bad outcomes. Let me give you an example: When I was in my thirties, back in the States, I was dating a woman by the name of Debra. Lovely woman, bright and charming. She was a nurse at a local hospital, with ambitions to become a Registered Nurse. We got along splendidly, loved each other, enjoyed each other's company, and the sex was good. She wanted to get married. I didn't. So of course, we eventually split up, and she became an RN, married someone else, and had a child.

I should have married her. But I foresaw that marriage would destroy my independent life, that children would chain me down financially, and that I would have to sacrifice part of my identity to be a part of a family. So, I didn't marry her. And now I live alone in Panama and have no experience as a father, no experience as a husband in a long-term marriage, no experience of the kind of love that grows because of being in a long-term relationship and working through problems as a couple. And since I'm dead now, and "life" consists of recreating experiences from the memories of my past life, I have no material to create that kind of love. I will never have that kind of love, *ever*, in my life now. I'm like a comic who goes on stage and has only heard one joke his whole life, so all I can tell is that one joke over and over. I'm sure I will create new women to meet. I'm sure I will have sex again. I'm sure I will experience infatuation and new love again. But I will never experience the kind of interdependent love that comes from forty years of marriage. If you don't experience something when you're alive, you can't experience when you're dead. It's just a fact of life... or rather, a fact of death.

I'm not being judgmental here. I understand that everyone, including me, makes the best decisions they can make at the time based on the information they have at that moment. Based on the information I had when I was thirty, marrying Debra would have been a bad move. Back then, I could foresee the price I would have to pay. I knew what I would lose. I thought I was exercising my free will based on a careful analysis of the risks and benefits of marriage. I was dodging a bullet, or so I thought.

And here's the paradox: I could not have made a different choice. I put my thirty years of experience into the analysis of whether to marry her or split up, and all the facts lined up on the "do not marry" side. To use my Go metaphor, I knew it would be a bad move. I had no choice but to say no.

But I was wrong. Because there is no free will. We make the choices we make based on our experiences. All the information that we have in our brains to make decisions is based on our experience, and that's *only* our experience—it's not any kind of truth. There is no truth to our decisions. Life is not a chess game or a Go game. We think we can foresee outcomes in the future, but we're only looking in a mirror of the past. We're only deciding to repeat our experiences.

I would have been a better person if I had married Debra, but I didn't. And thus, I became the person I am now. There's nothing wrong with that. It's just how life is... or was.

CHAPTER FIVE

I had returned from the store the other morning, and was walking up to my apartment with a bag of groceries when Joey—our crazy gringo—approached me and, for no particular reason, launched into another one of his paranoid diatribes:

"Do you know what the coronavirus has done to our civilization? It's put an end to democracy, that's what it's done. The Russians and Chinese started using digital face recognition to track people leaving their houses during the lockdown, and now the American government wants to use it to track where everyone goes all the time! In China, the people are required to carry their cellphones everywhere, so that the government always knows where they are. That's why they invented the virus, you know—to have an excuse to track us everywhere. It was invented just so they could grab more power. Look at what happened in Hungary, how that Orbán guy used corona as an excuse to become a dictator. The US helped the Chinese develop the virus in a lab, did you know that? That's when they added those extra RNA parts to target black people. It was all part of Trump's plan to get rid of minorities..."

"Do you want a beer, Joey?" I asked, reaching into my grocery bag.

"Well... it's not even noon yet, Robert."

"What does that matter if the world's coming to an end?" I said, and pulled out a can of beer from the six-pack I had bought. I held it out to him.

He paused for a second, then took the beer from my hand. "That's true. Yes, a beer would be nice. Thanks," he said and walked away.

That's my basic strategy with Joey: to give him alcohol when he goes off on one of his paranoid rants. I had read somewhere, years ago, that alcohol calms schizophrenics down. At the time I thought it was bullshit because alcohol calms everybody down. But over the years I noticed that the craziest people I knew always medicated themselves with alcohol. At any rate, it seems to work with Joey. When his conspiracy theories get too outlandish, I try to give him alcohol. It seems to calm him down, or at least shut him up.

As I was putting my groceries away inside my apartment, I began to think about conspiracy theories. They're so easy to fall into, so easy to believe, because, like our decisions in life, they're based on our *experience.* And our experience is always that someone or something is out to get us. And we have that experience because, in fact, bad things happen to us. They happen constantly. We stub our toe; the ATM eats our card; it rains when we forget our umbrella; the car breaks down; the job promotes someone else over us... Life is just an unending series of minor and major bad things happening to us. So, we naturally look for patterns to explain it—that's what our brain does. It looks for patterns. So if the water from your faucet tastes odd, and then one of your kids gets sick, and then someone tells you the city is putting fluoride into the water system, well voilà! The city is poisoning your child.

The perfect conspiracy theory contains three elements: First, it connects at least two dots from your experience of something bad; Second, the cause for the misfortune was done intentionally by some vaguely-identified person or group; And third, it's going to get worse, or at the very least, not get any better. For example, you apply for a job but don't get hired, and then later you learn that a person of color got the job, and then someone tells you that the city had implemented a new affirmative action program... well, voilà.

As an aside, did you ever notice that there is *never* a conspiracy theory about something good? No one ever pulls you aside and whispers, "Did you hear that the city is going to add new training for all its electrical repair linemen so that we'll have less problems with power outages? They got a grant from the feds, so it won't cost us anything. Yeah, I've got a friend on the inside who told me, but it's all hush-hush, so you didn't hear it from me."

One could argue that there aren't any positive conspiracy theories because nothing good ever happens, but the truth is that good things happen all the time. It's just that they're invisible. You never notice when something doesn't break, when something doesn't go wrong, or when someone doesn't let you down. No, conspiracy theories are reserved for bad things, or possible bad things, but mostly for bad things that are never going to happen. Ever notice that? All the dire predictions of the most popular big conspiracy theories never happen. (Ask all the people who built nuclear bomb shelters in the sixties.) That's not to say there's not evil in the world. Evil exists. Boy, does it exist. And that's not to say that some individual people don't spot a weakness in the system and, like Cassandra of old, are ignored when they warn us about it. But the fact that evil exists is not a conspiracy theory. And the fact that systems have weaknesses is not a conspiracy theory. Evil and systemic weaknesses are mostly the result of stupidity, laziness and selfishness; whereas a big popular conspiracy theory needs a mastermind, a superhuman villain behind the scenes pulling the strings, someone who's never caught. A good conspiracy theory requires a fiendish, intelligent but secretive person, or group, working in the shadows, like the Illuminati or George Soros, or the Federal Reserve, or the UN, or the Freemasons, or the Mafia, or the World Bank, or just simply the always-handy go-to villain: the federal government. To be clear, horrible events happen in this world, and people get away with individual murders and other horrendous shit all the time. But, the difference between real people conspiring to do BIG evil and the popular big conspiracy theories is that the real people are eventually exposed for who they are, whereas the conspirators in any big popular conspiracy theory are never exposed, never caught, and never punished.

Things rarely go as planned, and that fact happens to real conspirators as well. And the bigger the plan, the more things that can go wrong. Real people who undertake real conspiracies on a grand scale eventually are discovered. It may happen immediately, or it might take decades, and some of them might escape punishment, but eventually the facts come to light. Take a look at your big conspiratorial events: The great Gunpowder Plot of 1605 (where conspirators planted bombs to blow up the House of Lords in England) was discovered the day before the bombs were supposed to go off. Everybody knows how John Wilkes Booth was captured and killed twelve days after he killed Abraham Lincoln, but people forget that he had two co-conspirators—Lewis Powell and David Herald—who were supposed to assassinate Vice President Andrew Johnson and Secretary of State William Seward. Both of them failed to do so, and they were caught and executed. It took a world war to expose the Nazis for what they were, but the Holocaust was eventually revealed in all its horror for the world to see. The Ku Klux Klan conspirators who bombed the 16th Street Baptist Church in 1963, killing four young black girls, were eventually identified and convicted. The Watergate burglars were caught in the act; Haldeman and Ehrlichman went to jail; and Nixon had to resign the presidency. Osama bin Laden and his top organizers of 9/11 were identified, and all eventually either killed or arrested.

The bigger the conspiracy, the brighter the light that eventually exposes it. We read with morbid fascination about the downfall of Enron, HealthSouth, Tyco, Bear Stearns, Lehman Brothers, AIG, and WorldCom... but why are we able to read about them in such detail? Because their real-life conspiracies, frauds, scams, or plans failed and were exposed. And this is the main reason I am always skeptical of every new conspiracy theory—because I have a deep and abiding faith in the stupidity and incompetence of most people. And I have a bigger faith in people's inability to keep a secret.

I don't mind conspiracy theories so much. They abound in gringo-land. Norteamericanos have such a cultural distrust of government to start with, that when they become expats, their paranoia is unchecked, and their distrust increases tenfold. To live among expat gringos means you will be swimming in a sea of conspiracy theories. And it's not just Joey who spouts them—his theories are just the most ludicrous. But all the expats down here read them, listen to them, repeat them, and believe them. So I've heard them all: how the FBI killed Jeffrey Epstein; how cell towers spread coronavirus; how the US government is going to outlaw paper money; how Trump is a Russian mole; how Bernie Sanders is a Russian mole; how the IMF is planning to bankrupt all of South America; how the Chinese are going to build the new silk road to Africa and bankrupt the US; how gold is king; how gold is worthless... the list never ends. And I always have the same question for them: "If that's true, so what?" I don't say that out loud too often, because I don't wish to be rude to my fellow expats who are babbling these theories over a shared beer or two, but I always think it. Well, to be accurate, first I usually think, "What a crock of shit," and then I think, "If that's true, so what?"

I remember one time, a bunch of us expats were sitting together having a beer (which is a daily occurrence in this town), and one gringo—I think it was Ralph—was going on about how all the US government bailouts were going to lead to hyperinflation and cause the dollar to plunge, and how we all needed to just invest in gold, and that when the world economy collapses only the people with gold will be able to survive. For the briefest second I was going to open my mouth and say "So what? None of us has any money to buy gold with, so what difference does it make?" But luckily, I thought better of it and kept my mouth shut. Conspiracy theories for gringos are like hearsay and rumors—they are not offered for the truth of the matter, but simply to pass the time away, to have something to talk about while we sit and drink our beers.

However, I have to confess my own personal hypocrisy, which is that sometimes I propound these conspiracy theories when I write my vlog scripts for the *Solipsistic Times*. Sometimes my scripts just lightly touch on conspiratorial themes, like last week when I wrote a piece called "Why Cash is King—Keeping Your Inner Harmony with a Cash Emergency Fund." Nothing wrong with that... frothy, but practical. But sometimes I go a bit further. The other day, for example, I wrote a piece entitled "The Three Essential Oils You Will Need to Survive the Next Plague." Now, in the context of apocalyptic survival, you might think I meant motor oil or cooking oil, but I was talking about stuff that smells nice, like eucalyptus and pine. I forget which three smells I finally settled on, but the point of the vlog was something about building your immune system through aromatherapy. There's a specific structure to these types of scripts. First, I have to give it some historical reference. So, I name-dropped Ibn al-Baitar, the great Andalusian physician and botanist of the thirteenth century. Then I have to gently hit the paranoia button, so I copied some statistics about the frequency of pandemics from the black plague to coronavirus. Then I have to give it some legitimacy, so I quoted a recent science article on aromatherapy and the immune system. Then I made sure to talk about how "they" don't want this information out, so I threw in something about how Big Pharma wants to ban all forms of alternative medicine. Finally, I have to end on a positive note, so I finish up with some New Age mumbo jumbo about positive energy. Now, this vlog was a bit further out there than maintaining an emergency fund, but still... it had some scientific basis because, in fact, I had read some article on the phytoncides in the air around forests and their impact on monocytes and NK cells in the immune system. Just because I'm dead doesn't mean I'm not well read. So at least that vlog had some extenuated connection to science.

But occasionally, I just go full bore into the conspiratorial world. Usually it happens when I'm hungover, in a foul mood, and have a deadline to meet. For example, yesterday I wrote a piece entitled, "US Hedge Funds Created

Covid-19." It was a pretty crazed piece, but like I say, I was pretty hungover. I started off with the old rumors about the Covid-19 virus being created in a lab in China, except that I added the allegation that the lab was financed by a secret group of hedge fund investors. Then I quoted some statistics on how hedge funds had bought up all the foreclosures after the 2008 subprime collapse. Then I made up a story about how in the summer of 2019, hedge funds were looking to create another windfall like they had with those 2008 foreclosed properties... and voilà, I connected all the dots and posited that the hedge funds purposely released the coronavirus in Wuhan to see how fast it would spread, and then they intentionally brought it to the US on cruise ships in order to temporarily shut down the American economy to create all the foreclosures, so they could buy them up again just like they did in 2008 and 2009. (I claimed they brought the virus to the US on cruise ships because they had also shorted the cruise ship industry.) To make that sound less outlandish that American investors would intentionally risk human life, I reminded the listeners how American investors and companies collaborated with Hitler to build his Nazi killing machine, e.g., how IBM helped create the punch card number system for tracking Jews in the concentration camps, and how German war trucks were powered by Ford and GM motors. That's one of the requirements of a good conspiracy theory: At least two of the alleged facts in the theory have to be true. In this case, anyone can Google the fact that American investors and businesses were in bed with Hitler, and that hedge funds made a killing in the foreclosure resale market after the crash of 2008.

Still, it was difficult for me to keep a straight face while writing it. But I had a deadline, so I cranked it out and emailed it in. The editors at the *Solipsistic Times* seem to like my vlogs, and so I might as well make some extra money while I can...before *they* come and take it all away.

CHAPTER SIX

Lately I've noticed that some of Joey's crazy ideas must be rubbing off on Tom. I first noticed it about two weeks ago when the six of us were sitting around the picnic table in the backyard having a beer or two, as we do most nights.

I probably should first explain that this apartment building, like all apartment buildings in Panama, is a gated property, that is, there's a tall iron fence that surrounds the building, and there's concertina razor wire at the top of the fence. We refer to the property alternately as the Compound or sometimes the Green Zone, but the fact is, this type of fencing is normal throughout Central and South America. Why? Because anytime you have poor people, you have thieves, and if it's one thing Central and South America have an abundance of, it's poor people. When most tourists first come to Latin America, they are shocked at all the razor wire and iron bars on every window. They think they are in a war zone or some murderous slum run by drug lords. That is, until they take a ride through the ritzy neighborhoods and see that iron gates, razor wire, and bars on the windows are simply the norm on every house. It's not that Latin America has any more thieves than North America—it's just that Latin America has more poverty. If you leave a backpack unattended at the beach for more than three seconds, it will be stolen. It's just a fact of life down here. If some black plague or nuclear war were to turn the US into a third world country, you'd see the exact same behavior there. As Vladimir Lenin said, "Every society is three meals away from chaos." He was right about that.

Anyway, many apartment buildings down here were built with gringo tenants in mind, i.e., higher rent, but with Wi-Fi and air-conditioning. The more elegant gringo apartments have a swimming pool and a security guard. But our building is a bit on the cheaper side—no security guard and no pool. But we do have the requisite fencing and razor wire, and we do have an enclosed and shaded back yard with a nice patio and a picnic table. It's actually a large cement table with cement benches that easily holds six people. And every night, as the evening cools down, many of us gringos gather there to drink beer and talk. The talk is mostly bullshit, but we do it for the company (and the alcohol). Expat gringos will never admit this, but we are a lonely breed. Why? Because we're a self-selected group. The average expatriate never fits in anywhere, so they leave the States with the hope that there's some place in the world where they do fit in. And so, whenever expats meet each other, they do whatever it takes to maintain the illusion that "this place is *it*", i.e., the place where they truly belong, the home that they didn't have in the States, some kind of paradise that they alone have discovered. It isn't, of course, but that's the nature of a shared illusion, and woe to the gringo who violates that shared belief. So, we gather each night, drink our beers at the picnic table, and talk about how much better this is than sitting at a picnic table in Florida or California, or anywhere else in the world.

Anyway, as I was saying, about two weeks ago Tom, Ralph, Dave, Emile, Joey, and I were sitting there enjoying our beers when, out of the blue, Tom asked Joey, "Tell me about this blockchain thing and bitcoin."

A couple of us glanced askance at Tom, for the unspoken rule in our gatherings is never to encourage Joey in his conspiratorial ramblings. But Tom had already said it, and Joey rose to the occasion.

"Well," Joey started, "the thing you have to understand is that Satoshi Nakamoto is the man who created bitcoin, but no one knows who he is. He wrote this essay in 2008 describing how bitcoin worked, then he created the first blockchain. But then he disappeared. Maybe he never existed. Maybe the CIA and the US Treasury Department invented him as a way of injecting bitcoin into the world. But I think the CIA killed him so they could steal his bitcoin idea and replace paper money with electronic money that they could track..."

But Tom interrupted him. "Yeah, yeah, Joey, but what I want to know is, how does blockchain work."

"Oh that," Joey said. "Well... well, suppose that Villa Rosario—the entire town—only consists of ten blocks, but that everyone in that ten blocks has a computer, and that every computer is hooked into everyone else's computer, like one big Facebook page, so everyone's computer for all ten blocks is linked together in a chain, okay? And everyone's cell phone is also hooked into everyone's computer, okay?"

"Okay," said Tom.

"And suppose you have a bicycle and you want to sell it to me for one hundred dollars."

"Okay," said Tom.

"And suppose that one dollar equals one bitcoin. But suppose for some reason there are no more dollar bills or paper money in the world. But we can go onto our computers and you can sell me your bike for one hundred bitcoins. And I now own your bike. And all the computers in the entire town know that you have one hundred bitcoins in credit from selling me your bike. Now the next day, you go down to the grocery store and you load up one hundred dollars' worth of groceries in your cart and you go to check out, and the clerk says that'll be one hundred dollars, and you say I don't have one hundred dollars, but I have one hundred bitcoins in credit. So, you take out your cell phone and you transfer your one hundred bitcoins to the grocery store. Now the store has one hundred bitcoins in its account and you have groceries and I have a bicycle, okay?"

"Okay," said Tom.

"Now suppose," Joey continued, "later that same day, you go to the hardware store and you want to buy a power drill that costs one hundred dollars. And you take the drill to the checkout counter and the clerk says that'll be one hundred dollars, and you say I have one hundred bitcoins in my account, but when the clerk checks his computer—because remember, all the computers are connected—he says no you don't have one hundred bitcoins in your account because you spent your bitcoins at the grocery store."

"Yeah?" said Tom.

"Well, that's how the blockchain prevents fraud. Everyone's account for all ten blocks is connected like links in a chain. That's why they call it a blockchain."

"Yes, yes, but how do you make money on bitcoin?" Tom asked.

"Whaddya mean?" asked Joey.

"Bitcoins used to be worth pennies. Now they're worth thousands of dollars. I read how people are getting rich on them. How do you do that? How do you get rich on bitcoin?"

"That's not what they're designed to do," said Joey, raising his voice. "They were designed to prevent banks from making money by ripping off the little guy. But that was before the CIA killed Satoshi Nakamoto and took over his blockchain idea. Now investors are speculating on bitcoins as if they were pork belly futures. That's the problem with capitalism—it converts every good idea into a something you can make a casino bet on."

I thought this had become a pointless discussion, but evidently the group was interested. Dave spoke up. "I read that bitcoin was actually created not by a person but by a computer."

"Yes!" Joey shouted. "That's very possible, because the programming code for bitcoin and blockchain is so complicated that no group of scientists, no matter how bright, could have written it. Maybe CIA created a supercomputer so big, a form of artificial intelligence so huge, that it's gotten away from them, and it's now running the CIA."

"Wait a minute," said Tom. "Real people are making money off of bitcoin, right? I read where some guy in Atlanta, a few years back, bought seven thousand dollars' worth of bitcoin when they were only three dollars each, and now he's a multi-millionaire."

"Well, you can't do that now," Ralph interjected. "The cat's out of the bag."

"You could do it, if you knew when to short the bitcoin market," Joey said.

"Whaddya mean?" Tom asked.

"Well, right now, bitcoin is at an all-time high," Joey said, "but that can't continue. There are too many competitors. There's Ethereum, Litecoin, Monero, and Zcash. Bitcoin is bound to lose ground to one or more of them. If you knew when to short bitcoin against them, you could make a killing."

"I've never heard of any of those," Dave said.

Joey just shrugged and said, "They're worth millions."

"And how would you know when to short bitcoins?" Tom asked.

"You'd have to work at the CIA, because they are the ones controlling the whole thing," Joey said.

"I don't know," Ralph interjected. "I think the whole cryptocurrency thing is just a big scam."

The group was silent for a second. Then Emile, who I've always thought of as the voice of reason, spoke up. "Let's face it, gentlemen, the world is passing us by. None of us know anything about these new currencies—if, in fact, they *are* currencies—but in truth, I can't imagine that good old cash is going to disappear soon. How can you have corruption without good old cash?"

"But that's the point of bitcoins," Joey spouted. "It's supposed to be transparent; it's supposed to be corruption-free."

Emile laughed, "My dear friend, cash was invented because mankind needed a method to manage corruption. You can't do away with corruption via computer code. A certain amount of corruption is necessary to make the economy work."

"Corruption destroys the economy!" Joey shouted.

"No, no, I don't think so," Emile said. "I think corruption provides the fuel that powers the economy."

I looked over at Tom. His brow was furrowed. He seemed deep in thought. This would have been a typical maniacal, stupid, beer-fueled gringo evening except that I sensed something was wrong with Tom. I was just about to say something to him when Herald (who must have heard all the animated conversation from inside his apartment) came outside and walked up to the group.

"Sounds like y'all are having too much fun out here. Mind if I join the conversation? What are y'all talking about?"

I knew this was the beginning of the end of my evening. Joey answered him. "We were talking about bitcoin."

"Bitcoin, huh? Yeah, I have a cousin back in Oklahoma who's in the bitcoin business. But me, I made my money in the oil business. Now, oil... that's something you can always count on. I own a bunch of land in western Oklahoma, bought it for a song. Worthless acreage. Nothing grows on it except tumbleweeds, but the reason I bought it was because it still had the mineral rights attached to it. Most land in Oklahoma doesn't include the mineral rights, didya know that? When they struck oil in the Glenpool fields back in 1905, all these speculators realized that they could make a killing selling mineral rights, so they went door to door to all these poor farmers and offered them twenty or thirty bucks for the right to drill on their land. Those stupid farmers sold away all their mineral rights forever. Now all that land is littered with oil wells, even in the middle of big cities. You buy a house in Oklahoma and all you're buying is the surface property. You can drive through the neighborhoods of Tulsa today and see some big mansion with a huge oil well in the back yard, and I guarantee you that homeowner does not own that oil well. So when I found this patch of desert outside of Anadarko that still had the mineral rights, I pounced right on it and bought it. Two hundred acres. Now I lease it out to wildcatters who think they can still strike it rich. I've earned back what I paid for it a couple of times over."

I could see that Herald was going to hijack the conversation, like he always does. He was still standing because all the seats at the picnic table were taken, so I pretended to look at my watch, and then spoke up.

"You can sit here, Herald," I said. "I have a Skype appointment in a few minutes that I need to make."

I stood up and nodded goodbye to Dave and Emile. I had used this Skype excuse before when Herald showed up, and both Dave and Emile knew it was a ruse.

Herald took my seat. "*Thanks. Yeah, oil is the only way to make money, either by selling it, or buying it, or leasing land to someone else to drill for it, or selling the options to buy the mineral rights. I tell you one thing: a man who can't make money in the oil business in Oklahoma just doesn't know how to make money. Now my cousin Dewayne, he was dumber than a box of hammers. He didn't know jack shit about making money, but he knew how to drill for oil. He could put up a rig faster than any man alive. I used to pay him twenty bucks an hour to put up oil rigs, but then I'd rent him out to wildcat companies for fifty bucks an hour, and I'd pocket thirty bucks an hour all day every day for doing nothing, not even leaving my office. I remember one time...*"

And I walked away. As I implied earlier, I do not like Herald. But I'm never mean to his face, because I've got money riding on how long he'll stay, and when I win, I don't want anyone to say that I forced the outcome by being mean to him. So, I'm always polite. But I never hang around to listen to his bullshit braggart stories. I don't mind sitting and listening to the other gringos at the table talk about stuff they don't know anything about, but Herald always makes the stories about himself.

I really have no idea why I created him.

He must represent some horrible part of me.

Anyway, the next morning, I was out on my balcony, having my first cup of coffee with the sunrise when I happened to see Tom sitting at the picnic table down on the patio sipping at what looked to be his coffee. Tom lives on the first floor. We residents on the second floor have a balcony with a chair and a small table where we can sit and enjoy the view. But the residents on the first floor don't have tables or chairs on their patios, unless they buy them themselves. So, they tend to drink their morning coffee either inside their apartments or at the picnic table.

But in any case, there he was, sitting by himself. I had a box in the refrigerator that still had a couple of donuts left in it from a few days ago, so I went back inside my apartment and got the box and took it downstairs to the picnic table.

"Hey Tom," I said, "I have some leftover donuts, and I thought you'd might like to have one."

He halfway smiled thanks, reached into the box, picked one out, and just looked at it. He looked like he might have had a few drinks too many the night before, but I pressed on.

"Tom, what was all that last night about bitcoins? You got Joey all revved up."

He just shrugged. "I was just wanting to know how they worked."

I've known Tom for a long time. He rarely cares how anything works.

"Is something wrong?" I asked.

"Well..." He paused a second, but then said, "I got an email from my brother Ernie the other day, the diabetic one in Florida."

"I remember you telling me about him. Lost a leg, right?"

"Yeah, that one. Well, his diabetes has gotten worse and now the doctors want to remove his other leg. Evidently, he's got gangrene."

"Oh man," I said. "That sucks."

"Yeah. And his wife's dementia has gotten worse too. She's started wandering away from the house whenever his back is turned, and that's dangerous, because they live near the freeway. The police have had to bring her home twice this week. If he loses his other leg, he won't be able to care for her. He's been trying to find an Alzheimer's home to take her, but they're all so expensive. He'd have to sell his home to pay for them."

"What? Doesn't Medicare pay for nursing homes?" I asked.

"He doesn't know. He keeps hearing different stories from his friendsNot really," Tom said. "One neighbor told him that Medicare only pays for the first twenty days, then after that they would pay eighty percent for the next eighty days. But after that, he could be on the hook for the rest. And his wife could live a long time."

I thought about this for a second, and realized I knew nothing about what Medicare covered and what it didn't cover.

"Does he have any of that supplemental insurance?" I asked. "I forget what it's called."

"Medicare Advantage. No, he doesn't have that or any other kind of insurance. He's never was one to plan ahead. Now he's kind of fucked."

"I'm sorry, Tom."

"Yeah, ever since I got his email, I've been trying to think of some way to help him. I thought maybe if I invested in something like bitcoin, something that might skyrocket in value, that I could give him the money. That's why I was asking Joey."

"You know it never works that way," I said.

"Well, I had a friend who bought a thousand shares of Amazon at eighteen dollars a share back in 1998," Tom said.

"I don't know, Tom. We've all got a friend who lucked out," I responded. That's because people brag when they luck out. But the thousands of people who bought Enron stock when it was hot aren't talking about it now. People like you and me can't make a killing in the stock market, especially when we don't know what the fuck we're doing."

"I just want to help my brother."

"I understand, Tom, I do understand. How old is he?"

"He's sixty-nine."

"Well, Tom, you're down here. He's up there. You're not exactly in the best location to advise him. There must be someone in his area who can help him make these decisions. People up there would have more information on his options."

"Yeah, he's supposed to have a meeting tomorrow with some social worker woman from some community organization to talk about his wife."

"Well, maybe he'll have more options after that conference," I said.

"I just hate that someone would have to lose their home because they don't have enough insurance," Tom said. "He worked all his life to buy that property. It just makes me crazy. Joey always talks about health care being a human right, and lately I'm starting to believe him."

"Well, I can't disagree with him on that either."

Tom finally took a bite of the donut that had been in his hand the whole time that we had been talking.

"This one is kind of stale," he said.

"Yup. They've been in the fridge for two days."

Tom continued to munch on it. "Still, they're pretty good. Can I have another one?"

"Help yourself."

"You know," he said, "the problem is, I saw this coming four years ago. When Ernie retired, I told him he ought to sign up for extra insurance. So did his doctor. He's been overweight all his life, but he's never managed his diabetes well. Plus, he smokes and drinks a lot. I told him that the extra insurance would be a smart investment. But he said he didn't want to spend the money. He said the only way he could afford insurance would be if he gave up drinking. That was his favorite line. 'Insurance poor and sober' he called it. Shit, I wish I could go back in time and make him sign up for it. But I guess he wishes the same thing now. If only he knew then what he knows now."

"Yeah," I said, "I suppose everybody wishes they could go back in time and do things better."

CHAPTER SEVEN

The thing I said to Tom about going back in time to do things better got me thinking. I have to say that, being dead, I don't feel particularly connected to time. By that I mean that I don't experience time as flowing, as a continuous series of connected events. Time moves forward as it is supposed to do, but I experience my consciousness of time more like jumping from lily pad to lily pad, where I don't experience the jumping so much as I experience the stopping and looking back to the last lily pad I was on, and then looking forward to the next lily pad. It's only when resting on the current lily pad that I seem to be conscious of what's going on. Now, I'm not saying I jump through time like Billy Pilgrim. No, no. This is death, not science fiction. The events of time always have a logical, one-directional flow to them, one thing after another, even when disasters strike, because that's how the universe is designed. What I'm talking about is that my conscious state—my mental awareness of what's going on—seems to alternate between being in an alert state of intelligent awareness or being completely dimwitted. That is, I might find myself sitting in my chair at my desk staring out the window and thinking about taking a walk, and then, in what seems like only a few minutes later, I'm back in my chair staring out the window thinking about the walk I just took. I know I took a walk because I have distinct memories of which route I took; the smell of the Spanish cedar trees that line the road I walked on; the unusual large red and blue bird I saw on my walk; other people I saw also out walking; the sounds of cars in the distance; etc., and yet, the "now" that I experience is always "being back" in some place thinking about what has just happened.

Maybe the living experience this too, I don't know. But I don't think we're completely aware of things *while* they are happening. It's only after something happens that we're aware of it. The clearest example I can think of is sex. When we're having sex, it's intense, it's vibrant, it's sweaty, it's real... and then afterwards, we're lying there thinking: "That was wonderful." And we look back on it and we remember the smells, the tastes, the touch, the sounds, the thrill... but we're *remembering* it. I don't think we fully *experience* it while it's happening. It's almost as if a part of our brain shuts down when things are actually happening. Then we wake up a few minutes later and our brain tells us what happened. And if the sex was good, then the next day we find ourselves wanting it again, and we may seek out that same person again, and we may have sex again, and again our brains go somewhere else while we are in the midst of the sex, and we come to our senses afterwards, and find ourselves lying there panting and thinking, "That was wonderful."

I don't know. I could be wrong. Maybe that's just how it is after you're dead. Maybe the living actually experience things *while* they are happening. I don't quite remember how it was for me when I was alive. I only know how things are for me now, which is that I only feel conscious when I'm not doing anything, when I'm sitting still.

Maybe, when something is happening, there is *too much* happening for our brains to fully experience it, so we record it, so we can play it back later, so we can understand it. That would explain the "what I should have said was" moments that we all have. You know those moments— when there is some encounter between you and another person, and later you realize that what you *should* have said was X, Y, or Z, instead of what you actually said. Why does that happen? Your brain is the same during the encounter as afterwards. You have all the same information during the encounter as afterwards. Why was the exact moment of the encounter so different? Why was your brain so asleep at the switch that you couldn't think of that clever retort or whatever it was that you *should* have said? Well, maybe your brain was, in fact, asleep… overwhelmed, as it were, by the rush of stimuli during the encounter.

Or… maybe it's the opposite. Maybe your brain was in overdrive, reacting too fast to the event for you to realize the perfect thing to say. Maybe the encounter was stressful, and you stood there sputtering all kinds of nonsense instead of that one thing you should have said.

Is it possible to fully sense something when it's actually happening? Many philosophers and teachers throughout history have encouraged students in the art of not responding to experience. Carlos Castaneda encouraged "not-doing" as a way of feeling the world around us. F.M. Alexander described how "end-gaining" (or the automatic response to stimuli in human interaction) caused a person to continually repeat unconscious habitual patterns. He would have students practice simply not responding when given a command to respond. Alexander would have a student stand up from a chair and just stand there. And Alexander would say, "Now, in a minute, I'm going to tell you to sit down, but I don't want you to sit down. Just continue to stand." And he would wait a minute, and then he would say, "Sit down," and half of the time, the student would start to sit down. Even those students who knew the exercise couldn't help but make tiny involuntary muscular movements to start the sitting down process when they heard the command, "Sit down."

We are so conditioned by our habits. We think our habits serve us, but in fact we serve them.

The ancients knew this. In all spiritual disciplines, meditation has been used for centuries as the primary way to teach oneself how to not react to the constant onslaught of both external and internal stimuli and events.

Maybe if I took a folding chair with me on my walks, and sat down every couple of feet or so, to simply experience that moment, to interrupt the automatic action of "taking a walk", maybe then I would actually fully experience the walk as it was happening.

The only reason I dwell on these thoughts lately is that I'm trying to figure out what the point is in being dead. All my life I have believed (and I still believe) that there is a point to things, a "meaning" if you will, some organization to life, some system that underlies nature and existence. I'm not waxing religious here, believe me. I'm just talking about the interconnectedness of things.

And if there is a purpose to life, then there must be a purpose to death, or rather, to this "deathstyle" that is my existence now.

CHAPTER EIGHT

I ran into Tom a few days after my last conversation with him at the picnic table. He was in the parque central in front of the large Catholic church, sitting on a bench in the shade, just staring into space. I sat down beside him.

"How's your brother doing?" I asked.

He shrugged. "Not so good. He met with that social worker lady. I didn't understand any of the stuff he told me about the different types of nursing homes. It's all bureaucratic red tape bullshit to me. But it sounds like Medicare would pay for *him* to recuperate in a nursing home after his operation, but of course he can't leave his wife alone. So, he needs to recuperate at home. The social worker said that Medicare will only pay for a nursing home for his wife if she was recovering from some medical procedure like an operation, but Alzheimer's didn't qualify. There's also the Medicaid program, which I guess is different. The social worker said Medicaid would pay for a nursing home for his wife *after* they had depleted all their assets, which means he'd have to sell the house. So, like I said the other night, he's basically fucked. He really doesn't want to put her in a nursing home to start with, but he's not going to be able to manage her once they amputate his other leg. Evidently the social worker is trying to talk him into letting her find a nursing home they both could live in together. He had a different name for it, but it's basically a nursing home. If the social worker can find a place that will take both of them, she wants him to sell the house, move into the nursing home together, use the proceeds from the house to pay for the nursing home, and then she'll get them both on Medicaid when they run out of money so they can continue to stay at the nursing home together. But he doesn't want to sell the house. That's their home. They've lived there for thirty years. He wants to stay there. So right now, he's looking into having some kind of health aide person come stay at the house with them during the day to care for both of them. Then he'll just lock the house down at night so his wife can't wander off while he's asleep. But he's not sure how much a full-time health aide will cost."

I shook my head. "Shit, Tom. That sounds rough."

"Yeah, he's pretty depressed about the whole thing. I'm real worried about him if he can't find a solution to this. He made the comment to me that if he had known that this was how he and his wife were going to end up, he would have gotten ahold of some pills before they amputated his right leg last year and they would have had a little overdose party."

"Oh man," I said. "Do you think he would try anything like that now?"

"I hope not. He can't go anywhere without help now, so he's kind of limited."

"Does he have any other family besides you?"

"No, not anymore. They had a daughter but she died in a car wreck when she was a teenager."

"Shit," I said.

"Yeah, I'm the only family he's got left," Tom said. "I just wish there was some way I could help him."

I didn't know what else to say, so I just sat there with him for a while. A large black crow was splashing in the water of the nearby fountain. This particular park is the centerpiece of the town, and a lot of us, gringos and Panamanians alike, come here to sit in the shade of the tall palm and mango trees and think about things.

Finally, I asked, "Does he think this social worker is any good?"

"Yeah... yeah, that was the one bright spot. He said she really knew her stuff, that she seemed to really care about helping them."

"Well, her idea of both of them moving to some type of nursing home together kind of makes some sense," I said.

"I thought so, too. I told him that. Like I say, he just doesn't want to let go of that house. All his memories are there."

I understood that. Memories are all we have. They are what makes up life, what holds everything together, what gives it meaning, especially for me now that I am dead. Memories are all I have.

We talked about some other stuff for a while, and then I left him there and went over to the liquor store to buy some wine. I was out of wine at the apartment and needed to restock.

There is no wine industry in Panama—grapes do not grow well here—so all the wine is imported. But the people are poor, so the liquor stores only import cheap wine. But luckily for me, that includes a lot of Chilean wine, and Chile makes Carménère wine, which I love. So it's a win-win situation. I bought three bottles of inexpensive Carménère wine and started the walk back to the apartment building.

Carménère, if you didn't know, was one of the original six noble grapes of Bordeaux, France, before the variety was wiped out in the 1800s by the Phylloxera plague that destroyed seventy percent of the vineyards in France. Phylloxera is not a bacteria or a virus. It's a microscopic aphid that eats the roots of grapevines and kills the plant. There is no cure for it. Once it invades a plant, the roots must be ripped out and burned. Then the wineries must either plant all new vineyards (which take years to mature) or, if they cut the original vines from the roots, they can graft the existing vines onto new disease-resistant root stock and replant their vineyards with this vine. Phylloxera still strikes from time to time. In the 1990s, two-thirds of the vineyards in Napa, California, had to be replanted.

Anyway, the Carménère grape was completely wiped out in Europe by Phylloxera in the 1800s. But, through a stroke of luck, the grape had been taken by accident to Chile for planting—the accident being that the voyagers thought they were transporting Merlot vines (because the plants look similar). Carménère adapted to the sunny climate of Chile's central valley and thrived there. Chile now provides the world with this wonderfully delicious wine. I find its rich peppery chocolate-cherry taste very intoxicating (pun intended).

But I digress. The point is, as I was walking back to the apartment, I started thinking about Tom's brother. Gangrene has taken one leg, and soon it will take the other, in the same way Phylloxera ate away the roots of the noble Carménère vine in France. Carménère was uprooted from France, the only home it had known for centuries, and taken against its will across the ocean to Chile. Life is uprooting Tom's brother in much the same way, against his will, transporting him to an unknown future where he may or may not survive.

I suppose the metaphor only goes so far, because as Tom pointed out the other night, his brother brought some of this on himself by not managing his diabetes. But his wife certainly didn't bring her Alzheimer's on herself.

Despite the idea of karma, it seems that there are always some plagues out there, waiting to get us.

CHAPTER NINE

One of the reasons I bought the wine was that I've started to curtail my nightly beer drinking with the boys down at the picnic table. The reason I've done that is because Herald has taken to joining the group. And there are only so many times I can get away with using the excuse of a "Skype appointment" to immediately leave. So, if I see him down at the picnic table, I often just don't go down there. It's much more pleasant to enjoy a glass of wine alone up in my apartment than to listen to him yammer on about himself down there with the others. And, while I don't mind drinking beer if I'm sitting with other people, if I'm going to drink alone, I prefer wine. And if I'm drinking wine, I prefer Carménère.

But Monday evenings are different. On Mondays, Herald's not around. On Mondays, he attends a salsa dance class at some dance studio in the nearby city of La Chorrera. He only goes there to pick up women—he's bragged about that fact to us. He lets these poor Panamanian women think that he's just a lonely retired gringo (a lonely retired gringo with money) who might be good husband material. He'll let them latch onto him, and then bring them back to his apartment and have sex with them. He'll keep them on a string for as long as he can get sex from them, and then he cuts them loose. Some of the women he brings back here are pretty old, and some of them are downright unattractive. He doesn't care. He just wants someone to fuck. Of course, he's no prize either: short, fat, white-haired, bulldog face, loud, and obnoxious. But deceit is a two-way street. Evidently, one of these women ripped him off for two thousand dollars recently. Like most gringos, he had brought some cash with him when he flew down here to Panama. But he thought he was clever by hiding some of his money in one of those fake shaving cream cans that you can buy on Amazon. The can looks like a regular shaving cream can, but it's empty. The bottom screws off, and you can hide money inside. He put two thousand dollars in it, and kept it in his shaving kit in his bathroom. But gringos aren't the only ones who look at Amazon. And besides, all you have to do is shake the can to tell that there's something inside. Evidently, he brought some woman back to his apartment and had sex with her. She then excused herself to use the bathroom. After she left that night, he discovered his two thousand dollars was gone.

Maybe he was right that his dollars spoke enough Spanish. Maybe they were calling to her.

Of course, she disappeared from town right away. Two thousand dollars is like four months' pay down here.

But he keeps going to the Monday night dances, which is good, because it means I get to drink beer at the picnic table with my friends without worrying that he'll show up.

So anyway, on this particular Monday, I was down with the other fellows at the picnic table drinking beer. There was me and Tom, Ralph, Dave, Emile, and Joey. And Joey was unusually talkative.

"Over a million people die every year in car accidents. A million people! But no government tries to quarantine your car! You know why? Because cars don't mutate. You're not driving down the road when suddenly your Ford turns into a tank and starts blowing up other cars!"

"I had a Chevy one time that turned into a lemon," Ralph quipped.

"Viral mutations," Joey said. "I'm talking about viral mutations. Look, tuberculosis kills 1.5 million people a year. Influenza kills almost half a million. So does malaria. But you didn't see governments all over the world react to those diseases the way they reacted to coronavirus."

Emile spoke up. "But Joey, corona is more contagious.

It spread over the entire world in, what, forty days or something?"

"Exactly!" Joey shouted. "It's very contagious, but not very lethal. So why did all the governments get so draconian so fast? Why the sudden massive quarantines? Why did they shut down all those businesses?"

"Well, Joey, the bodies *were* piling up," said Emile.

"No," Joey said. "The governments could have taken one one-thousandth of the money they gave away and bought new hearses and dug new cemeteries and you would have never seen the bodies. No, the reason that all these countries went into quarantine so fast was because they knew something that they never told us."

Joey paused as if he was trying to organize his thoughts.

"Look, remember the Ebola outbreak in West Africa in 2014? The World Health Organization and the United Nations immediately declared it a threat to worldwide peace and security, and they immediately poured billions of dollars into fighting it. They sent doctors and food and equipment and medicine. It was a massive response. And why? Because Ebola is deadly. It kills up to ninety percent of the people it infects. So, the world's governments had to quarantine it immediately. Governments are no different than people. The only time we ever respond quickly to something is when we're really threatened by it. I mean, look at what governments all over the world did with corona. They shut their economies down! I mean, when do governments ever stop collecting taxes, stop economic growth? They told their people to go home, go inside their houses, and not come out, not pay rent, not pay mortgages, not pay taxes, not do anything! Why? Have you ever seen government act so fast? And not just one government, but all of the governments around the world... except for a few renegades. But think about it! How dangerous does something have to be for all the governments to mobilize in unison this way? We didn't do that with HIV, and yet it has killed 32 million people on this planet. We don't do that with tuberculosis, and yet we have a vaccine for it. We don't do that with malaria, zika, or dengue when all we'd have to do is spray for mosquitos. Think about it. Why such a massive, never-before-seen, worldwide coordinated effort against coronavirus when it's not that deadly? Why? Well, I'll tell you why...it's because they haven't told us the truth about coronavirus."

Joey actually had the group's attention at that moment.

"Okay," Emile sighed. "I'll bite. What did they know that they haven't told us?"

Joey pursed his lips and said, "They haven't told us that it mutates."

"All viruses mutate," Emile said curtly.

"Not like this one. This one mutates superfast. This one is mutating every day. It's never the same virus. It's like a giant computer trying to figure out a launch code to wipe out mankind. It's so contagious and it spreads so fast that if it mutates to something as deadly as Ebola, then it will wipe out all humans on earth in just a few weeks. What the scientists realized right away was that corona is very contagious and that it mutates superfast. That's why they have to keep updating the list of symptoms, because the symptoms keep changing. Even the way it kills keeps changing. First it was mild symptoms; then it was pneumonia in old people; then it was heart attacks in adults; then it was blood clots in young people; then it started infecting children. The virus is evolving into a killing machine. That's what they haven't told us."

The group was silent for a minute. Then Dave said, "I remember reading something about different strains of the virus."

"Yeah, but you don't read much about that anymore," Joey said. "They keep those stories out of the press now. They don't want the public to know the *real* truth."

"Just that it mutates?" asked Dave.

"No," Emile said, "I think what our friend Joey is driving at is that you can't make a vaccine against something that mutates that fast."

"Bingo-bingo!" shouted Joey. "Think about vaccines. What is the most common way to make a vaccine? You inject someone with a dead virus, and the body makes antibodies. Easy-peasy. Think about the vaccine for polio. Remember the controversy between the Salk vaccine and the Sabin vaccine? The Salk vaccine was a basically just dead polio virus. They injected you with it and you didn't get polio. Then Sabin came along with his vaccine which was inactivated polio virus. It wasn't dead, but it had been weakened to the point that it was inactive. The benefit with a live vaccine is that your body makes stronger antibodies to it. But the Salk vaccine still worked. It just didn't work as well as the Sabin vaccine, so the world switched over to Sabin. With corona, the scientists isolated the virus right away. They could have killed a bunch of it and made a vaccine from the dead virus, but no one did that. Why? Because they knew it wouldn't work. It wouldn't work because by the time they processed it and manufactured the vaccine, all the viruses in the world would have mutated to something totally different, and last week's dead vaccine would not protect you against this week's mutated coronavirus. That's why all the research went into those new types of vaccines—I'm not even sure they are technically vaccines—but they try to genetically modify your T-cells to create mutating antibodies."

"Mutant antibodies fighting mutant viruses?" said Emile. "I don't know about that. It sounds too much like a zombie movie."

So far, I had been listening to this entire conversation without participating, but at this point I finally spoke up. "Let me ask you this, Joey: You're saying that all of these scientists know that the coronavirus mutates rapidly; and they've told all the governments about how dangerous this is; and all the governments, well, most of the governments all over the world... decided to quarantine everyone to buy some time against this virus, right?"

"Right."

"And so... all the scientists know, and all the governments know, but they don't want to public to know, right?"

"Right."

"Do you think *all* those people, the millions of scientists and the millions of government officials would be able to keep a secret?"

"Sure."

"So how did *you* find out?" I asked.

"I figured it out! I read the news. I read the science. I know how to put two and two together."

"Don't you think someone somewhere would have said something?" I asked.

"And risk real anarchy?" Joey shouted. "If we all knew that Ebola was in the streets outside of our gates, would we be sitting here drinking beer? Fuck, no! We'd be up in our apartments loading our guns and counting our bullets."

"I see," I said, and decided to let it go.

I have no idea if Joey is correct or not. Joey has a new conspiracy theory every single day, so maybe eventually he'll hit the jackpot on one. It's like all the preppers hunkered down in all their underground bunkers in the hills of Idaho or Montana or wherever—eventually they'll be right. Eventually some apocalypse will bring the zombies or the government or the immigrants or whatever bogeyman they believe in, and all these bad guys will come pounding at their bunker door, but by then those preppers will all be long dead.

I bet that in 546 AD, just four years after the Plague of Justinian disappeared from the Byzantine Empire, some bright young scientist examined the pattern of how the disease had spread, and deduced that it was being spread by the ships that sailed from port to port in the Mediterranean; and he further deduced that there must have been something on those ships that caused the disease; and I bet that this bright young scientist looked at the recovering economy and all the trading routes that were starting back up again, and he predicted that the same disease would occur again in exactly one year; that this very same disease would break out again in 547, but this time it would be even worse. And if that bright young scientist told his friends, they would have accused him of being hysterical, but he would have been exactly right that the plague would return, and it would return stronger, and it would kill up to 200 million people; he would have been exactly right about everything except for the date. He would have been off by 800 years. That very same plague—which we now know was the bubonic plague—did return in 1347, and it decimated Europe. But this time it was not called the Plague of Justinian. This time it was called the Black Death.

So maybe Joey is right about everything except the date. Maybe eventually some virus will come along and mutate so fast that no vaccine or treatment will stop it, and maybe it will mutate into a disease that no human can withstand.

But... I don't worry about it. The coronavirus can't kill me because I'm already dead. But of course, I never share that information with my friends as we sit around the picnic table drinking beer. I don't want to be thought of as the crazy one. I'll let Joey keep that honor.

CHAPTER TEN

Joey is one of the craziest characters I know, but he's also one of the brightest. He's like a firecracker with a short fuse, always ready to burst into a fiery sermon on how the sky is about to fall, or why the economic bubble is going to collapse, or when the world is going to come to an end. And, like all good conspiracy theorists, he knows that *they* are behind it. But he's entertaining, because he always has a new theory. And I have to say, he does his research. I think he spends all day reading online conspiracy websites. I never seen him downtown. In fact, I've never seen him outside of the compound. I think he just rotates between his apartment and the small patio that holds our picnic table.

I think I created him out of several memories. Part of him surely must be based on this fellow I knew back at the university: Leon Fisher. Leon's body was completely covered with tattoos, all except his hands, neck, and face. If he wore a long-sleeved shirt, you'd never know he had tattoos; but in the summertime, if you saw him in shorts without a shirt, you would be stunned by all the color. His body was a marvel to behold. He had been a Grateful Dead devotee for years, just following them around, going to every show, and doing way too much acid. Every single tattoo on his body had something to do with the Grateful Dead, all in brilliant reds, yellows, blues, and greens. He had their logos in several places, plus the faces of all the band members, and blazing guitars and sunsets. His brain, however, was completely fried. He spoke fast, jamming his sentences together, but what he said just didn't make a whole lot of sense. He would jabber on about how he was in the witness protection program because of what he knew about the government and Patty Hearst and John Holmes and the Wonderland murders. Or sometimes he would say he was in the CIA. He just wasn't all there... in fact, he wasn't any there. But his family had money. The rumor was that his dad made a large contribution to the university, and they admitted Leon. He would bring copies of Grateful Dead song lyrics to class and just read them while the teachers lectured. The teachers knew never to call on him. He didn't seem to have any friends. It's hard to be friends with a crazy person. There was a certain intensity to Leon, a certain way he would jerk his head as if he just remembered that there was somewhere else he had to be. Eventually he graduated, although I don't know how. Maybe his father's money spoke to the university the same way Herald's money speaks to the whores. In any event, I heard years later he got committed to a psychiatric facility.

I think that I used Leon as a basis for Joey—for that certain intensity in his speech, and for his colorful conspiracies. But Joey is much more intelligent than Leon was, so I must have added in parts of Lewis McCullough. Lewis was a friend of mine years ago in Chicago. We both worked at this textbook company, and Lewis had the cubicle next to mine. He was one of the brightest, most well-read people I've ever known. But he had a fucked-up leg. He had to use this aluminum cane to get around, the kind that wraps around your forearm for extra support. If he had just had a bad limp, it wouldn't have been so tough for him, but his leg seemed to have a mind of its own. It wobbled wildly when he walked, which made him look spastic. He was horribly introverted because of it. He would never go to bars or anywhere to meet women. He lived alone and would read all the time. He could talk intelligently about so many subjects. Somehow, there's a part of Lewis in my creation of Joey.

Joey may be a phantom in my world, but the damaged people he's made from were real. I knew them when I was alive. They were real people, with real suffering.

I don't know why there are so many damaged people in this world. I never realized it when I was alive, but now when I look back, I seem to remember people, not for individual moments, but more for the whole arc of their lives. If I think of someone now, I see them first as children playing, then as young adults hoping for a future, then actually starting to make progress with their lives, but then their arc reaches some small zenith and starts to descend before they are ready, and then calamity hits them, or excess, or bad luck, or just the weight of their own limitations, and they have to endure the rest of their lives in a long slow descent.

Being dead, I now see what I was blind to when I had eyes—that we create the arc of our lives moment by moment while we're alive by each thought we think; and each thought is just a digested and regurgitated previous thought or experience; and that while we're alive, we lumber through each day, content with rethinking the same thoughts, chewing on our own mental cud. We never think that we can think differently by simply *thinking differently*. We never realize we can become unstuck by simply realizing we are stuck. We're not even cognizant that we are stuck. We have lost the ability to imagine a different life. Like some actor in a small-town play, we repeat the same lines night after night to the other actors, trying to make our performance appear fresh and spontaneous every night. But our thoughts and our tongues are tied and bound to the script. We are slaves to our permanent habits, which is to say, we are slaves to our personalities. While we're alive, we never break character, and never say something beyond the script. Our lives feel like a bad performance because we are, in fact, just repeating the same stale old lines. Thus, our lives become a predictable arc, and the gravity of endless repetition pulls us down.

We waste life while we're alive. And when we're dead, we can never get it back.

As I said earlier, the dominant quality of being dead is that there are no new experiences—you can only rehash the same old experiences over and over. This is what makes it so tragic that the living don't break free from their scripts and let themselves experience anything new. Their idea of doing something "wild and crazy new" is to do the same old thing in a new place. It's amazing to me how limited the living are, which is to say, it's amazing to me how limited I was when I was alive.

Which brings me back to my earlier question: What is the point of being dead? I think it must be connected to how and why I am creating these people in my world.

If death has any purpose, it has to be found in these people and this panorama of events that I am creating every day. It can't just be that this existence goes on forever, with me constantly regurgitating these memories up... There *has* to be some point to it.

Carl Jung said that "Whatever is rejected from the self, appears in the world as an event." I think that goes for the people in our world as well as events, because clearly I am creating these characters that inhabit my world—Joey and Herald and Tom and the rest—I know this because I recognize all of them as being assembled from all the different people I ever knew when I was alive... but why? What is it that I am rejecting from myself that causes me to create these people?

This question consumes me.

I remember one night, a few weeks ago, after another beer-soaked evening down on the patio, I was about to leave the picnic table and stagger up to my apartment, when Joey suddenly turned to me and said:

"What if everything they told us about science is wrong? Maybe all the theories have been twisted to keep us in the dark. For example, they claim there's no such thing as a perpetual motion machine, and yet the moon spins around the earth, and the planets all spin around the sun... for all eternity. Isn't that perpetual motion? If we had that knowledge, we could build cars that didn't need gasoline.

Maybe the oil companies and the car companies are hiding that science from us so they can just continue to sell us gas-guzzling cars. Maybe all the science they teach us has been twisted for political purposes. Take evolution, for example. If evolution really works, wouldn't that mean that stupidity is a better survival trait than intelligence? I mean, think about it. Did Darwin get it wrong or are they lying to us? No one reads Darwin anymore—we just read what they say he said. Maybe he didn't say 'survival of the fittest.' Maybe he said survival of the lowest common denominator. After all, there's more cockroaches than humans. They were around before we humans showed up on the scene, and they'll be here when we're gone. Maybe they just tell us that Darwin said 'survival of the fittest" in order to justify capitalism. Because if intelligence was better adapted for survival, there would be more intelligent people in the world. But there's not! In fact, there are less and less intelligent people, and more and more idiots populating the world. Maybe humans are evolving to be stupider. Intelligent people don't reproduce, but dumbfucks have tons of kids. That's why they're called dumbfucks—because they fuck all the time. Maybe intelligence was just a fluke, a mutant gene, a random event that evolution tried and then discarded because it didn't increase reproduction, like vestigial gills, residual nipples, and wisdom teeth. Maybe intelligent people will go the way of the dinosaur and the dodo bird."

As with most of Joey's rants, there's no point in really responding to him. Besides, I was pretty drunk and ready for bed. So, I just nodded and said, "You're probably right," and then went upstairs to my apartment.

It's so typical of Joey to say something so crazy and yet, somehow, his words get under my skin, and make me think for a few days. That little rant of his bothered me on several different levels.

The part about science being wrong really annoyed me because I absolutely believe in science. Any progress we've made as a species has been because of evidence-based science. And while I agree with Joey that religions, governments, demagogues and their promoters will always either distort or deny science, that doesn't make science itself wrong. In 1633, the great Italian astronomer Galileo was accused by the Inquisition of being a heretic because he believed that the planets revolved around the sun. There was a trial, and he was convicted. His books were banned, and he was sentenced to house arrest for the rest of his life. But the planets still revolve around the sun.

But what Joey said that really bothered me was the part about humans getting stupider. That hit a nerve because I have been thinking lately that the arc of my life didn't really amount to much. When I look back on my entire life, I think of how George Orwell described "what one invariably feels in revisiting any scene of childhood: How small everything has grown, and how terrible is the deterioration in myself."

My problem is, I can't see where I would have done anything different. I examine each phase I went through, the major decisions I made, the path I took, and each time, I conclude that I made the best decision I could have made based on the information I had at the time.

Which makes my earlier question all the more difficult: What is the point of being dead? And lately I've been wondering... maybe it's a chance to do things differently.

CHAPTER ELEVEN

I keep having this weird dream. There's fog in an open field, and a black crow that keeps diving into the fog. A rhythmic soundtrack plays in the background, like a click track in a music studio. I think it's music, but I can't tell. The crow seems to be diving in time to the clicking. I want to look around to see where the sound is coming from, but I can't seem to move.

And then I wake up.

This dream comes in the early morning right before I wake up. I've had it a few times now. Maybe it's the morning birds that trigger this dream. It's usually the sound of birds that first stirs me from sleep in the morning. Villa Rosario is still partly in the jungle, and this apartment building is on the edge of town, so we get all kinds of different bird sounds here. They start around four in the morning, singing to each other before the sun comes up. About an hour later the dogs start. I have no idea what gets them barking, but once something sets one of them off, they all join in. Most of the houses have dogs down here. They serve as another layer of home security. They live outside the houses, within the gates, barking at anyone who walks by, acting as sort of a low-cost motion-detector.

Our apartment building doesn't allow dogs, but all the houses across the street and beside us have dogs, so it's a cacophony of barking and howling and yapping every morning—or any other time of day or night—whenever they get started.

This morning I was aware of the birds singing, but I continued sleeping. Then the dogs started, and thoughts and memories started creeping into my head. This morning, I was having memories of Toledo, Spain, with its steep cobblestone streets that twist and turn, many of the streets too narrow for cars; and the stone buildings that hover over the winding streets, keeping them in a near-constant shade; the views of the Tegas River that flows around the city; the statue of Cervantes; the museum of El Greco; the wonderful food at all the outdoor cafes with the tables and chairs at all angles (because the streets are at all angles); the wine; the Roman ruins; the Arab ruins; the Jewish ruins; the Christian ruins; and countless little shops with the skillful gold artisans still producing damasquinados—those pieces of jewelry with intricate gold inlay—with techniques they learned from the Moors. I've always liked Toledo. I try and route every European vacation so that I can stay a couple of days there. It just happened to be my fate to be there when that fibrillation attack occurred. But I don't like thinking about that.

Toledo is a long way from Villa Rosario, and Villa Rosario is a long way from the United States. Strange the distance that life takes you. Life is travel, or at least my life has been. I assume that everyone's life involves distance. So, when I meet someone who has never traveled, I'm always amazed, stunned really, that someone would not travel. I remember a few weeks ago when I overheard Herald telling Ralph and Dave that Panama was the only country he had ever been to outside of the States. It was right after Herald had moved down here. I was up on my balcony, and he was sitting down at the picnic table bullshitting with Ralph and Dave.

"I tell you one thing, there ain't no better food than Oklahoma. I can get barbecue ribs in Beggs, Oklahoma, that are better than anything Kansas City cooks. Smoked for eight hours. The meat just falls off the bone. And steaks! I'm telling you, there ain't no finer steaks than in Okmulgee, Oklahoma. That's cattle country there. My cousin Dewayne and I bought

a couple of cows from this farmer in Okmulgee; then we had his friend Stumpy butcher them, and we aged them for couple of weeks, and drove them to Memphis, Tennessee, and sold them under the table to a bunch of restaurants. Doubled our money! I'm telling you, a man who can't make money in beef just can't make money."

"What about seafood?" Ralph asked.

"We got all the surf and turf you need right in Oklahoma, at any steak house you go to. And if you want fish, Red Lobster has shrimp and crab. Oklahoma's a progressive state."

"Where else have you traveled?" Ralph asked.

"Tennessee, Arkansas, Texas, Kansas, Chicago... boy I did not like Chicago..."

"No, I mean outside of the States," Ralph said.

"Just here. I read about all about Panama in that book, 'Mongering the World.' It said that Panama was the best place for expats like me, so I took the big plunge and came here. Best decision I ever made. Great climate, cheap beer, cheap women. Man-oh-man."

"Wait a minute," Ralph said. "Do you mean that Panama is the only other country you've visited outside of the United States? In your whole life?"

"Why travel unnecessarily? I did my research. Panama has the best whores, the best climate, the cheapest cost of living and the safest economy. I graphed it all out. Thailand's got great whores but it's too humid. Ecuador has got a cheaper cost of living but the women aren't that pretty. Colombia's got beautiful women but it's kind of dangerous. The Philippines have whores that can shot ping-pong balls out their pussies, but it's kind of unstable right now. Brothels are legal in Germany but the cost of living is so high... I researched every country, graphed it all out on an Excel spreadsheet, and Panama came out the winner. No one was more shocked than me, but facts are facts. Pretty women, low cost of living, stable country... You gotta hand it to Panama. They know how to do things right!"

At this point Dave spoke up, and basically asked the same question Ralph had asked, "Are you saying that Panama is the only place outside of the United States that you've ever traveled to?"

"Yup. I live in the best country in the world, so why go anywhere else? Well, except for the whores. That's the one thing the US is short on. Don't know why, really. In my daddy's day, there were lots of great whorehouses, but the women libbers shut 'em all down. So red-blooded expats like me gotta come down here."

I try and tune Herald out, but he has one of these booming voices that the over-confident always seem to possess. Even if I'm sitting up on my balcony on the second floor and he's down at the picnic table pontificating about something, I can hear every stupid word he says.

But, a few days after I talked with Tom in the park downtown, I happened to be out on my balcony, and I heard Herald talking to Tom down at the picnic table. This time I was glad I could hear him, because evidently Tom was still obsessing about bitcoin, and Herald was giving him what I thought was bad advice.

"You want to make money on bitcoin? Well, Tom, I probably shouldn't be telling you this, but I know how you can do that. My cousin Lawrence is a lawyer in Tulsa, but he doesn't practice law anymore. He don't need to. He started his own one-man hedge fund a few years back and now he's a millionaire. He trades in bitcoin. If you want to make money on bitcoin, I can put you in touch with Larry. You'll make money alright, I guarantee it!"

"I don't know, Herald," Tom said. "Joey was explaining to me how I have to set up a bitcoin account and create a bitcoin wallet on my cell phone, and that I'd have to file with the IRS. It all sounds so... complicated."

"Nah, you don't need to do any of that, Tom. You work with Larry, and you can buy bitcoin derivatives. You don't actually buy the bitcoin themselves; you invest in the bitcoin market. If bitcoin goes up, you make money. If bitcoin goes down, you make money. You ride the market like a boss

surfer. I tell you one thing: a man who can't make money on the bitcoin market, just can't make money."

"I don't understand."

"Well, let me explain it to you. You don't have to buy the actual bitcoins in order to invest in the bitcoin market. You can invest in the bitcoin market by buying bitcoin derivatives. Let's say you've got $500,000 to invest, and you think bitcoins are going to increase in value—and why would they not? Hell, they've probably gone up $100 just while we've been talking—well, you can buy $500,000 worth of the bitcoin market—that's called a derivative—and as soon as they go up a thousand dollars each, you sell your derivative electronically, and bam! It's instant because it's all internet electronic, and you've got instant dollars in your account. Your investment always stays in dollars and you get paid in dollars. Do that a couple of times and you got an easy hundred grand."

"Wait a minute, Herald. I don't understand, and besides, I don't have that kind of money to invest."

"Ah, that's the beauty of Larry's organization. He's a hedge fund—a private trading company. He only works with private clients. So you can leverage your investment. That's how the big banks all make their money—by using leverage. But they don't want the average investor to do that, so they make laws to prohibit guys like you and me to from using leverage to invest. But the big banks all do it. And private hedge funds companies like Larry's can do it."

"You've lost me. What's 'leverage' mean?"

"Okay, I'm going explain it to you in round numbers. Let's say one bitcoin was worth a hundred thousand today, but you think it'll be worth two hundred thousand in a month. So, you have Larry place an order to buy four bitcoins at one hundred fifty thousand each. But Larry writes the contract to have an execution date of thirty days down the road, which means you don't have to pay the seller for another thirty days, and he doesn't have to deliver the bitcoins until then. So, Larry puts that offer out on the market. And some bitcoin seller likes that deal because he'll be selling his bitcoins above

today's market price, so he accepts that offer, and now you have a contract. That contract is called a derivative. And that contract is worth six hundred thousand dollars, which is the value of four bitcoins at one hundred fifty thousand each. But in one month, that piece of paper will be worth eight hundred thousand, because it'll represent four bitcoins, which will have risen in value to two hundred thousand each. Follow me? Okay, so you hold that contract for a few weeks, while the value of the bitcoins is going up. But as soon as bitcoins go up to one hundred seventy-five thousand each, before the thirty days is up, you sell that contract for seven hundred thousand. You follow me? And then you pay the bitcoin seller his six hundred thousand, and the bitcoin seller delivers the bitcoins to the new contract owner, and you pocket a cool hundred grand for your trouble."

"But Herald, as I said, I don't have that kind of money!"

"Ah yes, but that's where leverage comes in. What's the name of that company you worked for back in Ohio? Pileson? Pullman?"

"Pearson."

"Right, Pearson. You told me you have a pension with them, right?"

"Yeah."

"Well, you use that as collateral. You sign a temporary assignment agreement with Larry, and whatever the value of that pension is, Larry will write a derivative contract for forty times that amount for you to buy bitcoin derivatives. And if you have life insurance or savings or own any land, you can lump the value of all that together and Larry can write a derivatives contract for forty times that total amount. It's so simple, and it's safe because, remember, no money changes hands until you sell your contract and deposit your profits. You never actually own any bitcoins; you're just trading these contracts, these derivatives."

"What if I don't know if bitcoins are going to go up or down in value?"

"That's easy. Just ask Larry. He's really knows the market. He's been doing this for years. Made a fortune.

Helped a lot of my friends make tons of money. I got his toll-free number in my apartment. You call him and chat with him. He'll explain it all you to you. Let me go get his number."

I watched Herald get up from the picnic table and lumber toward his apartment. I put my coffee cup down and quickly ran down to the picnic table where Tom was sitting and whispered to him, "Listen Tom, before you do any investing, please come talk to me, okay. I don't think I would trust Herald or his cousin."

Tom looked startled that he had been overheard, but nodded.

Just then Herald came out of his apartment holding a piece of paper.

"Hey, looks like we got a party going on. I was just telling Tom about my cousin Larry. He's a lawyer in Tulsa. Here you go, Tom. Here's Larry's number. You call him and he can give you all the details. It's toll-free."

Herald paused, gave me a once-over look, and started to say, *"In fact, this might interest you also. I was just telling Tom how to..."*

But I cut him off before he could get going. "Oh, I can't stay. I've got an appointment to pick up some special donuts I ordered at the panadería."

"The pana-what?"

"The bakery," I said as I turned to leave. "Gotta run or I'll be late."

I hurried back upstairs to my apartment, grabbed my coffee cup from my balcony table, and went inside to get my wallet. Then I made a big show out of leaving and locking my door, being sure to wave to Tom and Herald as I feigned a rush to leave to apartment building.

Of course, there was no donut order. I leisurely walked around town, but I was thinking about Tom and Herald. I like Tom. He has heart, but he's not the brightest bulb on the porch. Maybe he was just humoring Herald. But I felt some kind of obligation to make sure.

I recognize this tendency in me to insert myself into other people's lives when I think they are on the verge of

doing something stupid. It's a particular gringo affliction—
to think we know what is better for someone else. But I do it
anyway.

On the way back to the apartment, I stopped by the
panadería and bought a bag of their standard piña costillas,
or pineapple croissants. They were out of donuts, but I
needed something in a bag to bring back, just for effect.

CHAPTER TWELVE

I wouldn't exactly say that Tom has a drinking problem. He's an alcoholic, that's for sure, but as I said earlier, that goes without saying among expats down here. Tom drinks every afternoon down at the El Balcón bar, and "afternoon" by definition, can start any time after noon. So, I figured I would catch up with him there later that day.

So about two in the afternoon, I wandered down to El Balcón and sure enough, Tom was there, sitting at the usual table in the back corner. Luckily for me, none of the regulars were with him yet. I got a beer from the bar and walked up to him and sat down.

"So anyway, Tom, I couldn't help but overhear Herald pushing some bitcoin investment on you this morning, and it's none of my business, but in general, I think Herald's full of shit, and I wouldn't want to see you lose any money."

"Yeah, I know he's kind of obnoxious," Tom said, "but I talked to his cousin Larry today, and Larry's a bit more level-headed. He explained the whole bitcoin investment thing to me much better than Herald did."

"Tom, do you even know what a bitcoin is? It's a made-up currency. It doesn't exist. You might as well be investing in the outcome of a craps game. You can't hold a bitcoin in your hand. You can't buy stuff with it," I said.

"Well, actually you can," Tom replied. "Larry sent me a bunch of links to websites showing how you can buy stuff online with bitcoin. It's going to become the new world currency because it's not controlled by the banks."

I took a deep breath. Tom was in way deeper than I thought.

"Tom," I said. "If bitcoin is so great, why does everyone want your dollars for them? Any investment that wants your dollars means that your dollars are worth more than what they're selling. And if this cousin of Herald's is so smart, why is Herald living here in these cheap-ass apartments with us? How come Herald's not making millions on bitcoin?"

Tom furrowed his brow. "I hadn't thought of that," he said. "Larry said that lots of his clients had become rich off of bitcoin."

"Right," I said, "all his clients except Herald, his own cousin. Doesn't it seem odd to you that Herald is pushing this investment, and yet Herald lives with us? He doesn't have a car. He doesn't buy anything expensive down here. He talks big about Oklahoma, but what do we actually know about his life there? I mean, if you were rich, would you live in Oklahoma? We're here because of the cheaper cost of living. Isn't Herald here for the same thing?"

I seemed to have found a wedge into Tom's enthusiasm about bitcoin. So I continued to hammer at it.

"I mean, what's the cost of living in Oklahoma? How expensive can it be to live there? And yet he retires down here because he likes the *lower* cost of living. He's always bragging about how cheap it is to live here. And he also claims he comes down here for the whores, but you notice he never pays for them. He never goes to brothels, either here or in La Chorrera. He only hangs around dance studios and bars where he picks up stupid older women with his story about being a rich retired gringo."

I pointed over to the bar where a couple of the local hookers were having a coke, waiting for customers. "He doesn't even pick up freelancers like those two, and they're not expensive. And they're cute! So why doesn't he pay for any of the hookers he claims he loves so much? Because he doesn't have any money! He's all talk. Which is fine as long as you don't believe him. If what he told you about bitcoin was true, he'd be rolling in dough."

Tom's brow was furrowed, but his head was nodding up and down. I could tell he was thinking. "Yeah," he said, "you've got a point. I've noticed that when we're all down here drinking, he never buys a round. He lets everyone else do that."

"Uh huh," I said.

"But I really want to find a way to help my brother Ernie. We talk everyday now. He goes in for his operation the day after tomorrow. That social worker lady found some home health aide to stay with his wife while he's in the hospital and for a while after he gets back home, but Ernie says that he only has enough money to pay the home health aide for a few weeks. The social worker is still trying to line up a nursing home, some kind of assisted living place, that will take both him and his wife, but that means he has to put his house up for sale."

"I understand, Tom, I said. "That situation really sucks. But bitcoin is not the answer. You know what they say about something that sounds too good to be true. If bitcoin was a guaranteed answer, Herald would be rich... and he sure as fuck ain't rich. Maybe the best thing you can do for your brother is to simply continue to talk with him, to listen, to let him know you care. Maybe this social worker's plan for him and his wife going to a nursing home together is a good plan, the best plan for both his health and his wife's health."

Tom was nodding his head up and down again. I would have said more, but Dave and Ralph had come into the bar for a beer, saw us in the corner, and invited themselves over. Tom had not shared the information about his brother with them, and so the conversation turned to other topics. I finished my beer, had another one, and then went home to take a nap.

CHAPTER THIRTEEN

The next day I had a deadline to meet for the *Solipsistic Times*. I was trying to expand on an idea called the "New Hollywood Bland Diet—Lose Weight with Food that Doesn't Taste Good." But the words just wouldn't come. So I started going through my idea box for another topic. Whenever I get an idea for a vlog, I jot it down on a 3x5 card and throw it in this little box on my desk. Every idea I think of goes into my idea box. No censoring. My rule is that "no idea is too stupid for a vlog." Usually some idea will inspire me to write something. I grabbed the first twelve cards from the box and started reading:

> Russia's Campaign to Disrupt Your Chakras
> Vitamin B12—a Push-up Bra for Your Serotonin Levels
> Autoeroticism While Living in Your Car
> Jeffrey Epstein was Corona Patient Zero and Had to Die
> How to Monetize the End of Days
> How YouTube Can Help You Survive the Coming Apocalypse
> Using 5G to Control Your Roommate
> Subliminal Messages on the Weather Channel
> How Your Shoe Size Affects Your Mental Health
> The Dawning of the Age of Aquariums—Your Fish Tank and You
> What Your Wallet Says About Your Personality
> How the Government is Trying to Read Your Mind

I paused on that last one for a moment and started thinking how all conspiracy theories have to do with the idea of control. It's a central theme to every conspiracy theory—how "they" are doing something sinister, with the aim of either controlling you or controlling some aspect of life that affects you, like your money or your thoughts or your freedoms... and if it's one thing that gringos hate, it's the idea of being controlled. "You can't tell me what to do," is their battle cry, or at least their weekend protest chant, when they gather on the state capitol grounds after being told to do so by some social media outlet that they trust which is run by persons unknown to them. If there was enough space on the protest signs they carry, and if they could see the irony of the situation, they would write, "You can't tell me what to do unless you are the person that I want telling me what to do."

But I didn't feel like writing about government mind control, so I went back to the card about using 5G to control your roommate. And I started thinking about Wilhelm Reich and his "orgone accumulators"—those large plywood boxes lined with rock wool and iron. They were popular in the early 1940s. People would sit inside them to accumulate energy from the universe. Then I remembered how people in the sixties would meditate inside pyramid shapes to also collect energy. Evidently there's not enough energy in the world. And of course, there are the theories that the great pyramids in Egypt were energy accumulators that served as a gateway to other dimensions. That seemed like sufficient science for a vlog, so I started writing some gibberish about constructing a meditation room that would protect you from 5G radiation and enhance your orgone energy at the same time. Took me about ten minutes. Then I emailed that off to the editors. Another satisfying workday, and I still had my afternoon free.

But I actually think that ol' Wilhelm Reich was on to something. The fact is, there really *is* only so much energy to go around. And the other fact is, one does have to work to accumulate it. Now I'm talking about personal energy here, that kind of intense focus and awareness that comes once in a blue moon, when you have this crystal-clear vision, when you can think about your life and see it for what it is, and actually have enough energy to do something different. Those are rare moments, because as humans, well, we're just in a fog all the time. We think we are aware; we think we are conscious; but we're not. We're completely preoccupied with our little fog, completely dull, stupid, and inherently lazy. Someone has to enlighten us that it's even possible to be conscious. Maybe that's the single purpose of all spiritual disciplines, from medication to whirling dervishes: to accumulate some rarified focused consciousness.

Of course, I'm thinking all this as I walk downtown knowing I'm going to end up at El Balcón for at least one beer. It's an odd thing—to be thinking about my potential for a rarified consciousness while acknowledging—in the same thought—my own addiction. But I learned to embrace my inner alcoholic many years ago. I wish I could be enlightened, but I just can't. As Clint Eastwood said, "A man's got to know his limitations." History may have its stories of drunken Zen masters, but in reality, a drunk is always a drunk. I don't think it's possible to achieve detachment from the world while being attached to alcohol. The great Zen philosopher Alan Watts tried it. It can't be done. I recognize how my drinking defeats any effort I might make towards any (for lack of a better word) enlightenment. But I still drink.

My plan was to walk around town for a bit, to work up an appetite, because I wasn't quite ready for lunch, but then I passed by La Esquinita, and I saw Emile sitting by himself at one of their tables. La Esquinita is a tiny outdoor lunch joint, or "fonda" as they are known locally. A fonda consists of one person behind a grill and one or two outdoor tables, usually under a tin roof. In Costa Rica, they are called sodas. In Mexico, they are called taquerias. Here they are called fondas. The closest thing in the States would be a hot dog stand or a food truck.

La Esquinita is located on a corner, hence the name "esquinita". Like all fondas, you go up to the grill, give your order, and sit and wait while the cook prepares it. The cook calls out to you when it's ready, and you go to the counter to pick it up. After you eat, you return to the counter to pay. It's a very simple operation.

Anyway, Emile was sitting there at one of the two outdoor tables. I waved at him and walked up.

"Are you waiting for food, or have you finished?" I asked.

"I just ordered," he said, and gestured with his hand for me to join him.

I went up to the grill and ordered, and then returned to the table to chat.

"I've been kind of worried about Tom," I said.

"Yeah, I noticed he's been preoccupied. What's going on with him?"

I told Emile about Tom's brother, about the conversation I overheard him having with Herald, and about the subsequent conversation I had with him.

"Yeah, Herald's a conniver, alright," Emile said, "and an idiot. But Tom's an idiot too if he thinks he can make money on bitcoin. I heard him grilling Joey about it a couple of days ago. Talking to Joey about investments is like talking to a Catholic priest about sex. Joey was just filling Tom's head with nonsense, talking about how bitcoins are better than money because they're not controlled by government. What a bunch of crap! That's exactly why governments will never completely allow bitcoins. They don't want to give up their ability to manipulate currency."

"I'm afraid that Tom is going to give Herald's cousin his money," I said.

"He might," Emile said, "but if he does, it'll be his own doing. You warned him."

"I did. But Tom's desperate to help his brother."

Emile shrugged. "There's nothing you can do about that. The world is full of people who do stupid things for honorable reasons. All we can do is share our opinions. And you know how that goes: nobody ever listens to advice. Despite what the Bible says, we're not our brother's keeper—because our brothers won't let us."

Then Emile smiled and said, "And besides, you never know... he might get lucky and make money on bitcoin. Ha!"

Just then the cook yelled out to Emile that his food was ready. Emile got up to get his plate. My food was still on the grill.

I always liked Emile's way of looking at the world. It was sensible. He seemed to know his boundaries. I, on the other hand... well, when people I care about encounter problems, I instinctively worry that they *won't* be able to handle them without my help. So, I'm always intervening and offering my unsolicited advice. I've noticed that Emile never does that. He might ask a question or two, but he never gets involved in "helping" another person make a decision. I remember one time, about two years ago, this gringo named Brad moved down to our apartment building from New Jersey. He heard about our little gated paradise through a mutual friend of Ralph's. Brad had gone through a bad divorce about ten years previous. He always talked bitterly about his ex-wife, but like a lot of divorced guys, he missed being married. When he reached retirement age, he moved down here, lured by the stories of paradise, beautiful women, and legal brothels. He was similar to Herald in some respects—he spent his first few months down here drinking, chasing whores, and raising hell, but eventually the need to be married overtook him and he started dating this one Colombian hooker from one of the brothels. She was about half his age. All of us at the apartment building knew she was just using him for his money. We'd seen this racket a million times, but Brad was "in love" and believed that she was the one for him. He started dyeing his hair to look younger, wearing new clothes, and buying new clothes for her as well. He was always buying her expensive stuff because he "wanted to spoil her." He even got her name tattooed on his arm. She was milking him for two or three grand each month. First, she needed an operation that could only be done back in Bogota. Then her mom needed a new roof. Then her grandmother needed an operation. We all tried to make him see that she was using him—all of us except Emile, that is. He would join us at the picnic table at night and listen to Brad rave about what a princess this girl was, and then complain about how much she was costing him, and Emile would just listen and never say a word. The rest of us kept telling Brad that he was being played, but Emile just kept silent. I asked him once why he never gave Brad any feedback, and Emile just said, "He doesn't listen to all of you; what makes you think he'll listen to me?" He was right, of course. Brad didn't listen to any of us. He dated this woman for a few months, then moved out of the apartment building to go live with her in some dangerous section of La Chorrera. We never heard from him again. We all thought he might be dead. But after about six months, Ralph found out from his friend in New Jersey that Brad had moved back to the States... alone. That woman had taken every dime he had and then kicked him to the street. He was totally broke and too humiliated to contact any of us. He had his friend in New Jersey buy him a ticket so he could fly home.

Ralph and his other buddies in the apartment building were sad and frustrated about it, but Emile was nonchalant. "That was his destiny," Emile told me. "I don't interfere with another man's destiny. If Brad had sought me out, asked for my advice, that would have been different. Then I would have been drawn into his destiny. But that never happened. For whatever karmic reason, Brad is doomed to have horrendous relationships with women. He lost his shirt in his divorce, remember? That wasn't just a happenchance of fate—that *was* his fate. Did he learn from it? No. He just spent the next ten years of his life working like a dog to save up enough money to move down here, then meets this gold digger, and loses his shirt a second time. Hell, he might do it a third time. There's no stopping destiny. I might as well try stopping a speeding train. He was destined to have this train wreck. I was just privileged to stand on the sidelines and watch the explosion without getting hurt myself. Most of us are just witnesses to other people's train wrecks. Brad was going to do what he was going to do, and all your talking to him wasn't going to stop him. It was his destiny."

"Would it have been different if he had asked for your advice?" I asked.

"Of course," Emile said. "Then I would have been a character in the play of his life, maybe a pivotal role or maybe just a walk-on, but I would have been involved in his drama. But... he never asked me, so I wasn't in the cast. I bet if you asked him now, he wouldn't even remember me. I wasn't in his script."

Emile came back to the table with his plate. I was about to ask him whether he thought Brad and Tom were similar when the cook yelled out that my order was ready, so I got up and went to the counter. By the time I got my plate and something to drink, my thoughts about Brad had completely left my brain. Attention is ephemeral that way... at least, mine is.

"So, you don't think I should say anything more to Tom?" I asked when I got back to the table.

"Not unless he asks," Emile said. "It sounds like you've already pointed out the fallacy of Herald's pitch, that if his cousin's so smart why isn't Herald rich. If Tom can't put two and two together, he deserves to lose his money. Speaking of fallacies, have you heard Joey's latest theory about coronavirus? That it came from a meteor that crashed in China?"

"No, I haven't heard that one."

"Yeah, he found some obscure scientist in India or somewhere, who wrote some paper in some equally obscure science journal that claims that meteors transport organic molecules, proteins, and viruses across space. Supposedly, some meteor crashed in Wuhan, China, just before the coronavirus outbreak. He'll probably be ranting about it on the patio tonight. Better catch the show while you can, because you know Joey will be onto some new theory in a day or so."

I laughed. "Yeah, he's quite entertaining, alright."

"He's an interesting character," Emile said. "Did you know he used to work for the CIA?"

I laughed again. "No... did he tell you that?"

"No, it's true. He showed me several letters and old photographs. He was a CIA operative in Costa Rica during the Iran-Contra scandal. He oversaw the construction of a secret landing strip, where guns and drugs were flown in and out the country."

"You're shitting me! Joey?"

"Yup. Our little Joey. Kind of helps explain why he's so crazy. He showed me some old black and white photos of him with boxes of rifles being shipped into Nicaragua and kilos of coke that were flown out of Colombia. I wouldn't have believed it otherwise. Plus, he showed me these old letters from Langley, giving him instructions and stuff."

"Fuck, Emile. It's hard to imagine him coherent enough to follow instructions."

"Well, he was a lot younger back then. And I don't know if being coherent is a requirement for the CIA. Hell, they may have liked his wild talk. Or maybe that job is why he's so crazy now. He told me he used to swipe a kilo of coke from each shipment that flew in. He said he had all the coke he wanted, every single day, for months on end."

"Shit," I said. "That *would* fuck you up."

"Yeah, that it would."

"How long did he work for the CIA? I mean, was he a regular employee or just some contractor they hired?"

"I don't know," Emile said. "He was pretty vague on the exact relationship." Then Emile smiled. "For all we know, he could still be working for them."

CHAPTER FOURTEEN

I've always been a fan of science fiction, so I wanted to hear Joey's theory about a meteor bringing coronavirus to Earth. But I could hear Herald down at the patio that night, pontificating about how great the United States is, so I did not go down to join the group. If Herald were a perceptive man, he might notice that I am never there when he's there, or that I'm always in the process of leaving when he shows up. But I don't think he's that perceptive. And even if he is, there is nothing I can do about it. I do not like him, and I never deviate from my "La Brea Tar Pit Rule" of relationships.

The La Brea Tar Pits were formed at least fifty thousand years ago in California, when black pitch—a form of natural asphalt—began to seep up from the ground near current-day Los Angeles, forming deep pools of black sticky tar. Animals that were foolish or unlucky enough to step into the shimmering pools were trapped by the sticky liquid and drowned. Fossils of giant mammoths and saber tooth tigers have been excavated from these death traps. And for that reason, there's a giant wrought iron fence around the tar pits—to prevent unwary tourists or innocent children from meeting a similar fate.

I did not learn about the La Brea Tar Pits until junior high school. But I did know about tar babies much earlier. As a child, I read the Uncle Remus stories, and my favorite was the story of the tar baby. In those wonderful children's stories, Br'er Fox was always trying to catch Br'er Rabbit. (It is my belief that the famous road runner cartoons were based on these stories.) Anyway, in the story of the tar baby, Br'er Fox makes a sculpture of a baby out of black tar and places it in the road where Br'er Rabbit usually travels. The rabbit tries to interact with the baby and gets mad when the baby won't respond. So, the rabbit begins to fight with the baby and gets stuck in the black tar, whereupon the fox emerges from his hiding place and easily captures the rabbit.

In the original Uncle Remus version, Br'er Rabbit is able to talk his way out of being eaten, but in real life there is no escape from tar babies. Once you engage with them, you are stuck in the gooey mess of their lives. They stick to you like beach tar on the soles of your feet, contaminating your thoughts with their manipulative personalities and useless stories. The only remedy for tar baby people is to do what Los Angeles did with the La Brea Tar Pits—build a huge iron fence around them and never interact with them. You can't reason with them; you can't outwit them; you can't convince them to change; they are just gooey tar pits.

Which is why I avoid Herald. There's no other antidote to manipulative sociopaths. The trick, of course, is to spot them early and step aside.

Anyway, I could hear Herald blabbering on down at the picnic table. I peeked out my door and could see the usual crew down there, minus Tom and Ralph. I figured they must still be down at El Balcón. There's an odd tide of gringos that flows between the picnic table and that downtown bar. One or two of us start gathering at the back table at El Balcón at some point after lunch. Usually by four in the afternoon, the table is full. Then we start drifting away, one by one, usually to go back to our apartments for naps. The heat of the afternoon is a good time for naps, especially after a few beers. Then we normally reassemble at the apartment picnic table by six or seven in the evening, after everyone has had a nap and a bite to eat.

There's a couple of gringos who live elsewhere in Villa Rosario who occasionally join us in the afternoon at El Balcón. A few of them are nut cases, but most of them are decent fellows. But we never invite them to join us for the evening get-togethers back at the apartment building. The unspoken rule has always been that only the apartment residents are allowed to use the picnic table on our patio. This keeps the riffraff out.

So, in keeping with the La Brea Tar Pit Rule, going down to the picnic table was not an option, because Herald was there. I could have stayed in my apartment and opened a bottle of that nice Carménère, but I decided instead to walk down to El Balcón and see who might be there. After all, it was a nice evening for a walk.

So I grabbed my wallet and headed downtown. It's not a far walk because Villa Rosario is not a big town. And as I walked along, I began to think again about being dead. More and more it appears to me like a mystery. People always talk about trying to figure out the meaning of life, like why we're here on this earth—but that's nowhere near as difficult as trying to figure out the meaning of death... meaning, why I'm still here on this earth. I can only conclude that there are an infinite number of earths, as many as there have been people on the earth since the beginning of time. Because obviously, people die. I died in that hospital and my body was no longer alive. Since that happened in Spain, something had to have happened to my corpse. No one in the States or Panama would have paid for it to be shipped back to the Americas, so it must have been either cremated or buried in Toledo. Only my consciousness continues, in this dreamlike world that I call my life. Everything feels real, just like a dream feels real. In fact, everything feels absolutely real... but obviously, this world I inhabit can't be the world that I inhabited when I was alive. This has to be a different world, made up of recycled memories of the world I used to inhabit. But it's a world that must exist separate from the real world; it must exist on a plane totally apart from the world I used to inhabit. And if that's true for me, then it must be true for everyone—for everyone who has ever lived and then died, that their lives must continue on a plane of existence that is different from the world they used to inhabit; and that the world they now inhabit is different from my current world and different from the world of everyone else who has died. Which means that there are an infinite number of worlds all going on at once.

Thinking this thought made my head spin. I couldn't conceptualize it all. Then I wondered: Do I just continue to go on in this world, or will I die again?

That thought made me actually stop walking, and just stand there on the sidewalk for a moment. Can I die twice? What happens if I do? I thought about this for a moment, but then realized that I would not die again, because no one dies in a dream. You just go on. I felt more relaxed when I realized this, so I started walking again.

I returned to the central question: what is the point of being dead? As I said before, I am a believer in purpose. I don't mean divine purpose. I don't even necessarily mean intelligent or meaningful purpose. But there's always a certain organization to how everything unfolds, from the smallest plant to the largest black hole. Everything moves toward some unfolding, some event, some outcome... even if it continues forever.

I toyed again with the idea that maybe the purpose of being dead was to somehow become unstuck from the habitual patterns of life; that maybe it was some metamorphosis, some cocoon wherein something ugly is transformed into something more beautiful. But by this time, I had arrived at El Balcón, and my thoughts turned to more mundane matters.

El Balcón encompasses the entire second floor of the building it's in. The first floor consists of a bakery and a small clothing shop, both of which were closed for the day. A narrow and dark staircase leads from the street to the second floor. Once up there, I saw Ralph sitting by himself at the back table. I grabbed a beer at the bar and walked back to where he was sitting.

"May I join you?" I asked ceremoniously.

"Of course," Ralph said.

"Whatcha been up to?" I asked. And Ralph started to tell me about his day, how he spent his morning, where he ate lunch, some gossip he heard, etc. This is a ritual that gringos—and probably most people—play out a million times a day. It's a social ritual, a way of staying connected, a way to sit together and talk without actually saying anything actually intimate.

"And then for lunch," Ralph was saying, "I decided to try that new fonda next to the Chinese hardware store, the one that opened up last week. You know the one I'm talking about?"

"Yeah," I said, "I've walked past it. How was it?"

I was half listening to Ralph. Not because I didn't care—Ralph is actually a pretty decent guy, and I like him—and he was telling me about the food that the new fonda offered, and what the prices were, and how the service was. I was partly interested, but not really. I was nodding my head as if I were listening, but I became aware that an immense sadness was overtaking me. Maybe it was because part of my brain was still thinking about how life consists of being stuck in the same routines, and how death just seems to repeat those routines infinitely; or maybe it was because what Ralph was telling me was more of the same stuff I've heard forever. There are only so many fondas in this town, and they all serve the same thing; and the food is either good or it's not so good; and the prices are either cheap or expensive; and the service is either good or it's not so good; but it's all the same. It's always the same. I looked around El Balcón, with its black ironwood walls, and the other patrons hunkered down at their tables, and a few freelancers at the bar, and it's always the same. Then I looked back at Ralph, and he was saying how he liked the food at this new fonda and he would go back again, and I was nodding my head, but I was thinking maybe I had spent my whole life building wrought iron fences around everyone, as if everyone was a tar pit, a hazard to be avoided.

Is it possible to break out of our patterns? To actually become more authentic? I was still nodding my head, and

Ralph was finishing up his story, and then there was this pause in the conversation, and I felt that sadness again, and I decided I had to do something different—anything different—so I asked, "Do you ever miss the States?"

I could tell Ralph was a bit surprised by my question, because obviously, it was a total non sequitur to his story about the fonda, but it wasn't a totally crazy question, given that we were both expats sitting in a bar in Panama, so he thought about it.

"Yeah... yeah, sometimes I do."

"What do you miss about it?" I asked.

"Oh, I dunno... I miss the cleanliness, the organization, the regularity of it all, the fact that people have to pick up after their dog shits on the sidewalk, and the fact that you can go to a restaurant and trust that they're not handing you the menu with the higher gringo prices on it. I miss being able to get a good hotdog and see a baseball game."

"What made you decide to leave and come here?" I asked.

Ralph looked away. "Oh, the usual reasons, I guess. Before I got married, I used to come down here a lot for the, um, sportfishing, you know, and I always liked it here. That was years ago, of course. But then, after I got divorced, I started thinking about Panama again. By then, I was getting close to retirement, but I knew I couldn't afford to retire and stay in the States. So I thought, why not move down here? I made a few trips to make sure I wasn't crazy, but it seemed like a smart move."

"How long were you married?"

"Hmm... nine years."

"Kids?"

"No. She had two grown ones from a previous marriage."

"Do you still stay in touch with her?"

"Not really. We send each other Christmas emails, mostly to see if the other is still alive, I think."

I smiled. "Yeah, I understand that. I have friends back home that I send emails to for that same reason, to make sure they're okay and still alive, and also to let them know I'm still alive."

"You know what's funny?" Ralph said. "Last Christmas she attached a photo of her and her new husband to the email. I could barely recognize her. She's aged so much. It shocked me, because I always picture her the way I remember her back when we were married. I still remember her that way. I had to delete that picture. I don't want to think of her as old."

"Did you send her a picture of you?"

"Hell no! I don't want to ruin whatever image she has of me!"

We both chuckled over that. Just then, Dave walked over with a beer in his hand. He must have come into the bar while Ralph and I were talking.

"Hey," Dave said and sat down. "You two missed quite a show on the patio tonight."

"Why, what happened?" Ralph asked.

"Joey and Herald almost got into a fight. Emile had to actually physically separate them."

"What?" Ralph and I both said at once.

"Oh yeah, it was great," Dave said. "Herald was going on about how great the US economy was and how great Trump had been for the economy, and Joey started ranting about how the US had become a dictatorship run by corporations and the CIA, and then Herald said 'if you don't like it, why don't you leave?' and Joey said that was the stupidest thing he'd ever heard because obviously he did leave and that maybe Herald ought to go back if he loves it so much. Then Herald called him an anarchist and Joey called Herald a pussy, then they both stood up to fight, but Emile jumped between them and told them both to shut up. It was great! Best thing I've seen in weeks."

"Wow," I said. "What happened then?"

"Well, Emile lectured them both about how, as American expats, they have to all make an effort to get along and not antagonize each other, especially when they are both drunk. Shortly after that, both Joey and Herald went back to their apartments. Emile said he was going to turn in for the night, and I came down here."

"Was Tom there?" I asked.

"No, I haven't seen Tom in a few days," Dave said.

"I saw him this morning at the liquor store," Ralph said. "He told me he wouldn't be at the patio tonight because he had stuff to do."

"I gotta say, I was impressed how fast Emile moved," Dave said. "If he hadn't jumped up and gotten between those two, they would have started hitting each other."

"I wonder what it'll be like at the table tomorrow night," Ralph said.

"Well, I'm definitely gonna be there to see," said Dave.

CHAPTER FIFTEEN

But Herald wasn't there the next night. It was just Dave, Ralph, Joey, Emile, and me. Tom didn't show up either, although Ralph said he had seen him at the liquor store again.

I finally got to hear Joey's theory about coronavirus originating from a meteor. Joey was in rare form, fueled by a lot of beer.

He started off with: "You know that all life evolved from viruses, right? Viruses are what started evolution. Without viruses, we wouldn't be here. It's a well-known fact. Originally, Earth was just a rock, just a rock in space. But suddenly viruses appeared. Tiny life forms with ribonucleic acid... RNA. That was the start of evolution! But where did *they* come from? You can't evolve RNA from rock! Well, viruses came from the same place that the rock came from—from outer space! Outer space is full of cosmic dust, constantly moving around, and tons of it falls to Earth. They've analyzed this dust with electron microscopes, and it's full of polymeric hydrocarbon particles—that's the stuff of viruses!"

"I'm not following you," Ralph said. (This was a common refrain when Joey was on a roll.)

"Okay, let me explain it this way. Do you know what most dirt is made of? Skin. Dead skin. Most dirt is made of tiny dead skin cells that we humans and animals are constantly shedding. If you take a piece of dirty laundry and put it under a microscope, you would see that the dirt that is on the clothes consists of millions of flakes of dead skin caught between the individual threads of the cloth. The weave of the cloth acts like a fine mesh, catching these dead skin cells as they constantly flake off of our bodies. If you don't believe me, Google it! You'll see. Almost a hundred percent of dirt is organic matter, mostly dead skin cells. But those dead skin cells are evidence of live people, right? Well, if you put cosmic dust under an electron microscope, what you see are thousands of polymeric hydrocarbon particles. Those are dead viruses. That's evidence of live viruses in space."

"And where do you get this cosmic dust to analyze?" Emile asked.

"They gather it on the space station. It's one of their main scientific research projects—to try and figure out the origin of life."

"And do they find any live viruses in this cosmic dust?" Emile then asked.

"Of course not," Joey said. "Any viruses exposed to the sun, especially the intense sun outside of Earth's atmosphere, would be killed immediately. But viruses that exist inside of meteors would be protected from the sun. If a meteor made it through the Earth's atmosphere without burning up; if it hit the Earth and broke open; all of those live viruses would be expelled out into the air for miles. That's how life began on Earth. It was seeded with viruses from outer space. And that's how diseases get here, too. Like the coronavirus. It's an established fact that a meteor hit the Wuhan province in China in October of 2019. The Chinese government tried to cover it up. They confiscated any photographs that people took, took their cameras too, and put those people in jail. Any journalists in China that reported on it simply disappeared. But there are satellite images of it hitting the ground. And some pieces were smuggled out to an astronomy lab in England. There, they were able to analyze it."

"And?" Emile said.

"Well, it was hushed up, of course! No government wants to tell their citizens that some alien virus has infected them."

"So what proof is there that this meteor brought coronavirus to Earth?" Emile asked.

"Well, look at what happened. Look at how all the world governments started cooperating with the same shutdown protocols. Have you ever seen world governments cooperate so fast? All with the same party line? Once the Chinese figured out that this was an alien virus, they clued in all the big banks, and the banks then pressured the world's governments to fall in line."

"So, there is no proof?" Emile said. "No actual scientific proof that coronavirus is from outer space?"

"Just Google it!" Joey shouted, exasperated. "You'll see a bunch of scientists have supported this idea. But as soon as they do, all the bigwig medical organizations shoot them down. Well, guess who funds those medical organizations? Big banks, that's who."

"I see," Emile said.

During this exchange, I was thinking of the story of how Joey got into a fight the night before with Herald. I could tell that Joey was getting agitated, and I didn't want this evening to escalate.

"Want another beer, Joey?" I asked, holding out a cold can to him.

"Yeah... thanks," he said.

"Ralph was telling me he tried that new fonda over by the Chinese hardware store," I said to Joey in an effort to change the subject. "He said it was pretty good. Have you tried it?"

"No, I don't eat at fondas. Too many germs, and I don't know what they put into their food. I do my own cooking."

Dave spoke up and asked Ralph, "How was it, Ralph?"

"It was pretty good," Ralph said, and launched into the same story he had told me the night before. Joey sucked quietly on his beer, and my mind drifted to other things.

I suppose age has jaded me. I used to read the news of the world voraciously. Now, I avoid it whenever possible. I remember, years ago, the news consisted of *facts*, and the nightly newscasters would just read the news to you in a matter-of-fact voice. But there doesn't seem to be any factual basis to newscasts anymore. They should replace the phrase "nightly news report" with the "nightly *can-you-believe-this?* report." I do listen to Joey's rants because they amuse me. Plus, I know that I created him. So I'm somewhat curious as to what that part of me is trying to say to me... but ultimately, I don't care where whether the Chinese covered up a meteor crash, or whether viruses come from outer space, or whether the big banks control all the governments. It's all the same to me.

I finished my beer. I waited politely until Ralph finished his story about the fonda, then said my goodbyes and head upstairs to bed.

CHAPTER SIXTEEN

I had that dream again. The black crow was diving into this heavy fog as if he was hunting something. He would dive straight down, disappear from my sight, re-emerge from a different part of the fog, fly up, and then dive again. And there was that strange drumming again, more like a tapping, like someone hitting the metal edge of a snare drum. I couldn't tell where the sound was coming from. I tried to turn my head, but my eyes seemed locked on the crow.

I awoke again thinking of Toledo. I opened my eyes and looked around my small apartment. The morning light was sliding through the windows and making its usual pattern on the wall. Judging from the height of the pattern, I guessed it was about five a.m. I could hear the birds outside. I closed my eyes and thought more about Toledo. I remembered how the narrow and twisting dark streets would all converge onto some huge plaza, bathed in sunlight, bigger than a football field, a plaza lined with restaurants and souvenir shops.

Toledo is a fascinating city, full of history. I don't know why I chose to die there. Maybe we don't get to choose where we die. But if I had to die somewhere, I would pick Toledo.

Toledo is the perfect fortress city, located in central Spain, about forty-five miles south of Madrid. It sits high on a rocky hill, overlooking the Tagus River, which flows on three sides below it. The Tagus flows all the way west through Spain and Portugal to the Atlantic Ocean. Whoever controlled Toledo controlled transportation and trade on the Tagus. First it was ruled by the Romans, further back than 50 BC. When Rome fell in 554 AD, the Visigoths made Toledo their capitol. Then in 711, the Moors conquered Spain and made Toledo a vibrant regional center. In 1085 King Alfonso VI of Spain took control of the city. Toledo then became the capital of Spain until 1561, when King Philip II moved the capital to Madrid.

Although its history contains many episodes of violent conquests, it also contains centuries of peace, when Christians, Muslims, and Jews lived together in cultural and economic partnership. There are Christian churches in Toledo today that are housed in older mosques designed by Jews. There are synagogues constructed by Muslim craftsmen. The painter El Greco lived in Toledo. Miguel de Cervantes, the author of Don Quixote, was a frequent visitor to the city. The museums and churches of Toledo house paintings by Goya, Rubens, and Velázquez. It's just an amazing city.

I think certain places have their own unique magnetic energy. Maybe it's the earth beneath the place. Or maybe what we feel about a place is the energy of the builders and craftsmen and artists that survives in the architecture and the art of a city—maybe those forms and images convey something to us as we walk the streets. I don't know. I only know that Toledo seems to hold some mystery for me.

Then a thought occurred to me as I lay in bed: I wondered if I had created Toledo... If I created all these people in my world, it would stand to reason that I must be creating the places, too.

I lay there and thought about this for a moment. I finally decided that no, I did not create Toledo. It was a real place when I was alive. It exists in my memory because I experienced the reality of it. If I went back there today, it would be a dream of course, something I would be re-creating. But it would be a re-creation based on memories of a real place.

Those thoughts reassured me. After all, we all need some touchstone in our lives, something that we know is real and constant. Maybe that's the true function of memory—to connect us to those real people and those real places that kept us sane all those years.

My very last memories of Toledo are, of course, not pleasant. I only have fragments of them now: me standing in the street pretending to gaze into a shop's window while I desperately tried to catch my breath; me in a cab going to a medical office building where I hoped I could find a doctor; the doctor listening to my heart with a stethoscope and saying the Spanish word *fibrilación* and then giving me an EKG; me checking into a hospital where they looked at the doctor's note and my EKG printout and gave me a bed immediately; then different doctors and nurses talking to me; me and my bed being rolled down to some basement for the night, a room full of other old people, separated by white curtains; how hard it was to sleep with the drip feed in my arm. It's all a blur now, but it's a blur made up of individual memories. There doesn't seem to be any continuity to the flow of time in my memory of the last few days in Toledo.

I thought about this for a few minutes more. The light coming into my little apartment was much brighter now. It was time to get up.

CHAPTER SEVENTEEN

The rainy season has started this month, which means our evenings at the picnic table are sputtering to an end. Some days are just cloudy, but if the rains do come, they usually come in two waves each day: one downpour from one to three in the afternoon; then a break with few hours of muggy heat; and then a longer downpour that starts at six in the evening and lasts well into the night. The first downpour becomes a great excuse for gringos to gather at El Balcón for a beer to "wait out the rain," but the second downpour puts an end to any outdoor picnic table drunkfest at the apartment building.

The past two weeks has brought this weather pattern, and as a result I've been rather out of the loop for a number of days. I was mostly tied up with working on a new series of vlogs for the *Solipsistic Times* on "How the Deep State will Force all Van Lifers to get Vaccines" and "How to Go Stealth" to prevent this... um... obvious infringement on your rights, or whatever. Anyway, working on this series kept me busy most afternoons, so I wasn't able to get down to El Balcón as usual. And all of the evenings when I was free, got rained out. So, I hadn't seen the other gringos for over a week. But I finished my vlogs this morning, and the skies looked only partly cloudy, so after lunch today I headed down to El Balcón to catch up on the news from the tribe.

When I arrived at El Balcón, I could already see three of my fellow inmates sitting at the back table. I grabbed a beer at the bar and headed back there. There was Emile, Ralph and Dave sitting quietly at the table. They seemed a bit glum. I pulled up a chair and sat down.

"Hey guys, what's been going on?" I asked.

"Tom's gone," Emile said dryly.

"Whaddya mean?" I asked.

Dave looked at Emile and said, "Tell him."

Emile sighed and said, "Well, you were right to be worried about him. Evidently, he signed over all his retirement money to this cousin of Herald's."

"What? When did this happen?"

"About a week ago," Emile said. "Some kind of speculation deal where he was buying bitcoin futures. I don't know the details, but for the first couple of days he was ecstatic because bitcoin was shooting up in value."

I looked at their faces. I could tell that the outcome was not good.

"Then what happened?" I exclaimed.

"Don't you read the news?" Ralph asked. "The bitcoin market took a fucking nosedive this week."

I must have had a confused look on my face because Emile said, "It dropped so fast that whatever dark web bitcoin exchange Tom was using did a margin call on his investment. He didn't even know what a margin call was. He got wiped out."

"Where is he?" I asked.

"He went back to the States yesterday," Dave said.

"What?"

"Yup," Dave said.

"And Herald?"

"Gone into hiding, it seems," Emile said. "No one has seen him since this happened."

"And the sick thing," Ralph added, "is that bitcoin bounced back up today."

"He had no business getting involved in something as speculative as bitcoin," Emile said. "And definitely no business going all in the way he did." Then Emile looked and me and said, "You warned him. He was just stupid."

I sat there stunned. It was true that Tom was not bright, but he was a decent guy. I felt horrible and wondered if I should have done more to stop him.

"He lost everything?" I asked.

"Well, he still has whatever cash he had down here," Emile said. "And he still has his Social Security check. It's not much, but it's still intact. But everything else he had is gone. I think he even pledged some land that he had inherited from his mother."

"And somehow, Herald's cousin convinced him to take some advances on his credit cards too," Ralph added. "I didn't think that was legal, but somehow he did it. Now he has to pay those back."

"Or declare bankruptcy," Emile said. "I told him he needed to talk with a real lawyer when he gets back to the States, to see if he can sue this cousin of Herald's. The whole thing stinks of a fraud to me."

I looked at my beer. "I need something stronger," I said, and stood up and went to the bar to get a whiskey. This was too much to take in at once. How could he have been so stupid? Why didn't he listen to me? Why hadn't I followed-up with him and made sure he was safe? I really thought I had gotten through to him when we had our little talk. I wondered if anyone else at the table had tried to talk him out of it.

I returned to the table with a shot of whiskey and had a sip. The taste burned my mouth, but somehow seemed to help me.

"So... Herald's disappeared?" I asked. "Completely?"

"No one knows where he is," Dave said. "He hasn't moved out. You can look yourself. He left his blinds open. You can see all his stuff is still there."

"I think he ran off as soon as he realized that Tom had lost his money," Ralph said. "He's just waiting until the coast is clear before he returns."

"Maybe he's shacked up with some new girl from that dance club in La Chorrera," Dave said.

"Well, in any event," Emile said, "he has to reappear at some point. As you say, all his stuff is here."

"Unless he just grabbed his passport and ran to the airport," I offered.

Emile looked away for a second and then said, "No, I don't think he's the type to do that. He's very particular about his possessions. He wouldn't leave stuff behind. He'll show up again."

Ralph nodded his head. "Yeah, I agree. I think he's gone into hiding. He knew Tom was looking for him. He just ran away like the little chickenshit he is."

"Tom was looking for him?" I repeated.

"Well, Tom was pretty upset," Emile said. "I think that's when he realized he'd been had—when Herald disappeared. That's when it finally dawned on him that he'd been fucked over."

I took another sip of whiskey. "Fucking shit," was all I could say.

CHAPTER EIGHTEEN

I've mentioned that our apartment building is on the edge of town. And Panama is still, for the most part, jungle. On the back side of the property is a field, and just below that field, the jungle begins. That's where Herald's body was found. A few days after Tom went back to the States, some guy from the neighborhood was dumping trash out in the jungle when he discovered Herald's body wrapped in plastic and covered in about an inch of dirt. Evidently, someone had tried to bury him, but the recent rains had washed away most of the dirt.

According to the police, he had been bludgeoned to death. They said the back of his head had been caved in by some large weapon. They theorized that someone had come up behind him and struck him with something like a baseball bat, not once but multiple times. That's all any of us could get out of the police.

There was an investigation, of course. But that's not saying much in Panama. Some detectives from the DIJ (Dirección de Investigación Judicial) came to the apartment building and interviewed us all, one by one, but that was about it. Nothing ever came of it. First of all, the locals down here don't care if another gringo gets killed. Second, we gringos never cooperate with the police. So, it was a stand-off. As far as I could tell, no one even told the detectives about Tom and how he had lost his money to Herald's cousin. It turns out that when the police asked if we could think of anyone who might have a motive to kill Herald, we all independently mentioned the fact that some woman he met at that dance studio in La Chorrera had stolen his money. None of us knew her name, of course.

It might have been different if we had all liked Herald, but no one did. If the police wanted to assume that this woman told her friends that Herald had money and that maybe some of them came to Villa Rosario to rob Herald, that was fine with us, and fine with the locals too. The locals always prefer to blame any crime on hoodlums coming over from La Chorrera—it helps them preserve their idea that Villa Rosario is more of a Christian town than other places.

However, we gringos quickly deduced that he hadn't been robbed when someone from the US Embassy came to collect his valuables. One of the embassy's main functions down here—one of their *only* functions—is to gather any dead gringo's possessions and ship them back to their relatives in the States. Emile, Dave, and I helped the fellow from the embassy inventory the contents of Herald's apartment and box them up. That's when the police turned over Herald's wallet to the embassy guy. The wallet had been in Herald's pocket—that's how the police identified him when they found him—and his money was still in his wallet. His apartment keys were also still in his pocket, and all his other valuable possessions, like his computer, passport, spare change jar, TV, etc., were still in his apartment. He hadn't been robbed.

You would think that such a crime would have been the central topic of conversation among us gringos every time we got together as a group, but it was barely mentioned. I mean, there was a lot of shock and talk initially when the body was discovered, but as soon as it was clear that Herald had been murdered, we all shut up about it whenever more than two of us were together. Emile and I talked a lot about it when it was just him and me together, and I think Dave and Ralph did, too. But if the four of us were gathered down at El Balcón for beers, no one said a word about it. I think that was because none of us really knew for sure who had done it, so no one wanted to say anything that might suggest it was one of us. We all assumed that Tom was the culprit. But there was the fact that Joey had had that fight with Herald. Tom certainly had a motive, but Joey was crazy enough to be unpredictable. Ralph was close friends with Tom, and everyone knew he was pissed about what Herald's cousin had done to Tom. And then there was the fact that I had won the hundred-dollar bet because Herald was killed almost six weeks to the day after his arrival. Everyone agreed that the bet was how long a gringo would last, not how he would go, so I got the money. So, whenever the four of us were together as a group, there was this unspoken common delusion that if we didn't speak about it, things would just go on as if it had never happened. And if it was a clear night and we were sitting at the picnic table and Joey joined us... we *definitely* didn't mention it.

However, as I say, Emile and I did talk about it privately. I remember one conversation we had over lunch downtown the day after the embassy guy had taken all of Herald's possessions.

"Well, any US detective would immediately suspect Tom," Emile was saying. "Despite the twists and turns that TV crime shows always focus on, in real life it's almost always the person with the strongest motive. Tom lost his entire life's savings—that's a pretty fucking strong motive."

"Yeah, but I just can't see Tom doing something that violent," I said. "He barely had enough energy to get through his day. He spent all his time either worrying or drinking. He didn't seem to have the capacity to get angry."

"I don't think anger was the motivation," Emile replied. "I think it was identity. He didn't have much money, but he sure identified with what little he had. He was always talking about his little pension like it was a child he had fathered and raised. Plus, he was very attached to his brother. When he lost his money, he lost his ability to help his brother. Herald took away his identity. Without an identity to ground you, there are no morals to obey, no right or wrong. I think once he realized his money was gone, he simply had nothing to lose by killing Herald."

"I don't know, Emile. I can see Tom going a little crazy, but when you talk about crazy, Joey's in a class all his own. Ever since you told me that he used to work with the CIA, I've seen him in a different light, a darker light."

Emile gave a laugh and said, "There's more shadow than light in Joey, that's for sure. But if I were a betting man, I'd put my money on Tom."

"Hell, maybe they *both* did it," I suggested. "Herald was a fat dude. That's a lot of dead weight—pun intended. I don't think one man could have carried a dead body of Herald's size out of the apartment complex, over that field, down that hill into the jungle. Both Tom and Joey are lightweights. But both of them together might have been able to do it."

"Well, that's a thought," Emile said and laughed. "Let's ask Joey the next time he joins us for beer."

"Yeah, no," I said. "Let's just let it slide."

"You know," Emile added, "the other possibility is that it *was* a local, some panameño who had a grudge against Herald, some guy he pissed off, or maybe even some woman he used then threw away. You never know. He had a way of pissing people off."

"Yeah, that he did." I was quiet for a moment, then I asked, "Has anyone been in contact with Tom?"

"Not that I know of. I asked Ralph, and he said he had decided not to contact Tom. He told me he would prefer not to know who killed Herald. He didn't want Tom saying anything that would change that."

"Yeah. I get that," I said.

And I did get that. Now that I didn't see Herald every day, now that he wasn't around to irritate me, now that he was out of my conscious awareness, I just didn't care anymore. It was like his very existence had just evaporated. At first, I kind of felt sorry for him, that he ended up his lousy existence with someone coming up behind him and swinging an object at the back of his head so hard that it crushed his skull into his brains. But then I remembered that he never was alive to start with. He wasn't someone that I knew in my life when

I was alive. He was someone I created in this afterlife. He *never* existed. His life didn't go on after he died because he had never been alive. Once I remembered that, I stopped feeling sorry for him, stopped thinking about him.

Of course, I did have to think about what his death meant. By that I mean, I did have to wonder what I was trying to tell myself. If I created Herald out of some memory, or some disowned part of myself, and then I arranged that he be murdered by some unknown person or persons... why? What was the purpose, the message, the point of that? That stumped me. I just couldn't figure it out.

CHAPTER NINETEEN

The rainy season always wears me out. It lasts six months or longer down here, starting gradually in late April with just an occasional shower, but then slowly adding more and more water every day. By the time August rolls around, we only have five hours of dry daytime each morning to do shopping or walk around in muggy sunshine. By late September, the thunderboomers rattle the apartment building all day long, taking away our electricity when lightning blows out the town's transformers one by one.

I don't mind the water. Everyone wears shorts and waterproof sandals and walks with an umbrella. That's the norm. I can deal with the water. It's the lack of color that depresses me. Every afternoon the sky becomes a swirling mass of different shades of gray and black. The hard rain knocks all the flowers off the bushes and trees, and obscures the lush greenery. Everything looks like a watercolor painting that has been held under water. All the colors run. Everything takes on a gray mantle. I get depressed.

For years, Europe has been my escape. Every year I would pack my travel knapsack and leave during the worst three rainy months in Panama and fly to Europe for their wonderful dry summers and cool autumns. I had my packing down to an art, with special clothes that I only took to Europe, with my special travel laptop, my extra battery charger, my specially designed toilet kit, etc. Everything I needed all fit into my small travel knapsack. I was a model of efficiency, the epitome of gringo organization. I would study the travel books for weeks during the early rains of May and June, mapping out my route so I would always see someplace new, learn something new. But I would always end up in Toledo. All roads led to Toledo. I still don't know why. Maybe it's everyone's destiny to have a particular place to die, like in that famous story *Appointment in Samarra*. I don't know. I have accepted that there are just some mysteries I don't understand, and why we are fated to die in a particular place is one of them.

But this will be the first year in six or seven years that I haven't gone to Europe during our rainy season. I've certainly thought about it. I've flipped through my travel books. I've watched some travel videos online. But ever since I died, I just haven't been able to muster the energy to plan out an actual trip. Maybe that's the design of death—you die somewhere and then go back to your "home" to spend the rest of eternity... kind of like a nursing home for dead souls. I don't actually think that's the design, because I do want to go back to Europe. I intend to go back to Europe. I want to see Toledo again. But I just have to wait until I have enough energy. Maybe next year. But for now, I just have to endure the rainy season here.

Luckily, there is El Balcón. Everyone needs a sanctuary, a place of repose, a womb, a cave, a hiding place. And if it is comfortable, and has alcohol... well, so much the better. Let the rain beat down. Let the thunderboomers shake the outside walls. Every table has candles and matches if the power goes out. The bar is well stocked. Known customers don't even have to bring money—they can run a weekly tab and settle up once a week with the owner. It's the perfect place to practice endurance, to practice waiting... and in my case, to practice forgetting.

One of the perplexing aspects of being dead is that I forget that I'm dead the instant that anyone talks to me. I've tried to keep the awareness of my particular state of non-existence in my head when someone approaches, but as soon as they open their mouth, my brain focuses on them and what they are saying, and any consciousness that I am dead and that the whole conversation is a total illusion simply flies out the window. It's only after the person leaves, when I sit alone for a minute or two and ask myself "Now what was I doing before he walked up?" that I remember that I was sitting there being aware that I was dead. It happens anytime someone interacts with me. I think it's because they *look so real*. I've tried not looking directly at them, or not speaking right away, or biting the inside of my lip to keep my concentration on the fact that I am dead and that I am creating this person who appears in front of me... but it's no good. Within two to three seconds, I have forgotten that I am dead and I'm interacting with them, or reacting to them, or thinking what an idiot they are. It happens every single fucking time. Most of the time, I find this phenomenon maddening. But at least once a day, I am thankful for it; I embrace it; I submit to it. Because, let's face it, being dead is lonely. And so, I head down most afternoons to El Balcón where I know there will be other people to help me forget my loneliness. As I did earlier today.

As I stepped through the door on the second floor of the bar, I paused for a minute to let my eyes adjust to the low light. El Balcón was constructed of a local species of ironwood. Ironwood is naturally dark to start with, and over the decades, the wood has aged and turned completely black. The bar and bartender are located across the main room, over near the balcony, where there is sufficient light that you can see your drink and your money, but the table where we gringos usually gather is in the back where the light is dim. I glanced over to the corner and saw Emile sitting there. I ordered a beer from the bar and went and sat at the table.

"Joey grabbed me before I left the compound," Emile said as I sat down. "He wanted to talk about Tourette's Syndrome."

"Tourette's Syndrome? Really? What's his deal with Tourette's Syndrome?"

"He told me that the only people in the world who speak the truth are those people with Tourette's Syndrome,"

Emile explained. "He said that because they have no filter to what they say, they can never lie."

"Emile, I've heard people with Tourette's Syndrome. A lot of them just shout obscenities and make grunts or screams."

"Yes," Emile said. "That was exactly what I said to Joey, but he insisted that those sounds were the only truth in the world, that they were the true reflection of our animal nature. To be honest, I don't know why I waste my time talking to him. He's just so crazy."

"You know, I used to think that, Emile. But lately I've been wondering if his crazy talk is all an act. I know there's a little bit of madness in everyone, but Joey's madness sometimes seems a bit... predictable, a bit staged. If he sees us at the picnic table or just coming into the compound, he always has some opening line, always something crazy on his lips, but sometimes it seems prepared to me."

"Really?"

"Yeah. I was talking to Ralph the other day. You know how Ralph has the apartment next door to Joey? And the walls in our building aren't that thick, right? Anyway, for some reason we were talking about Joey, and Ralph told me something interesting."

"Yeah?"

"He said he never hears Joey talking to himself, *ever*."

"So?" Emile said.

"Well, I've known lots of people who are off their rocker, Emile, people who are drunks or crazy, and they *always* talk to themselves, especially the paranoid ones. But Joey never does. Ralph says he never says a word to himself. He just spends all his time on his computer, doing God knows what, but he's online all day and night. And I hadn't really thought about it until Ralph pointed it out, but it's true. Every time I happen to pass by Joey's window, I can see him hunched over his laptop, staring intently at the screen, oblivious to the world. For a crazy person, he's pretty focused."

"Maybe he's getting his secret coded messages from his overlords on Jupiter," Emile suggested.

I laughed. "Yes, well, that could be. But the next time we gather at the picnic table—if this goddamn rain ever stops—the next time we're out there and Joey comes out and starts on one of his wild yarns, watch his eyes. Notice how he watches everyone. He's not just babbling crazy theories—he's actively watching every single person's reaction. I could be wrong, but sometimes I get the impression that he's monitoring his performance. And it makes me wonder whether he simply wants us all to think he's crazy."

"You think it's all an act?" Emile asked.

I had to hesitate on that question. "Well... I don't know about it *all* being an act... He has been talking crazy ever since I've known him, I'll give you that. But on the other hand, you know those CIA types. They never stop pretending to be somebody else. They're always undercover, always maintaining a separate identity."

Emile smiled and nodded, and then said, "True, but we *all* do that to some extent, don't we? all of us, every day?"

I was going to reply, but just then Dave and Ralph came up to the table with a pitcher of beer.

"Man, we got here just in time," Dave said. "It's *pouring* out there! I'd much rather be pouring in here."

Emile laughed. I glanced over past the bar to the balcony. I could see sheets of gray rain coming down at an angle. Dave and Ralph started talking to Emile about some gringo who got robbed over in La Chorrera. But I was still mulling over Emile's first and last comments to me. Maybe Joey was right that people with Tourette's are the only ones who speak the truth, because the rest of us certainly do create lies every time we open our mouths. I remember reading Erving Goffman's *The Presentation of Self in Everyday Life* more than fifty years ago and thinking he was being way too cynical, but now I realize he was just being accurate. People are always lying. Shakespeare said it more poetically in 1599: "All the world's a stage and all the men and women merely players." Either way—the actor going through his part or the person slogging through daily life—it's all a performance; it's all lies. Every word we utter is just an attempt to impress whoever is on stage with us. It's an ensemble cast, each of us taking our turns, giving our little speeches, advancing the scene, developing our characters... I looked around at my fellow players: Emile, Dave, and Ralph. Not a bad group of castmates, I guess. But still, such a second-rate play. I looked over at the extras: the bartender cleaning shot glasses, the two hookers drinking cokes and chatting between themselves... all there for scenery. No lines for them today. I looked at the props: the chairs, the other tables, the walls. It all seemed so artificial.

I took a sip of my beer. *I need to get a grip,* I told myself. I should look on the bright side—that I would not even be aware of how hollow my existence was if it wasn't for the fact that I was dead. Being dead just highlights how much of human activity is totally pointless. But it also creates the need to do something about it. I've been telling myself for months that if I could just figure out why I'm dead—what the *purpose* of being dead is—then maybe, just maybe, I could unlock all this energy and get back to living life the way I used to... or at least the way I wished I had. When I look back at the arc of my life, it seems so constrained, so logical, so *normal*... and then when I look at my existence now, it seems so... well, so dead. My daily existence now is no different that Emile's or Ralph's or Dave's. I rotate between El Balcón and the picnic table, between the fondas and my own small kitchen, between being awake and asleep. If space aliens were observing the four of us, they would conclude we were without any conscious awareness beyond innate habit. If they watched the pattern of our daily activities the same way humans bend over and watch ants trudging in a line from the anthill to the bar for liquid nourishment and then in a line back to the anthill, they wouldn't give a second thought to kicking our anthill to dust. Surely, we were made for more than this.

I briefly consider announcing to my four castmates the truth of my existence: that I died in Toledo and have returned, like Lazarus, to Villa Rosario. But I remain silent. Unlike television or theatre, you can never break the fourth wall in life. The show must go on.

CHAPTER TWENTY

All the moisture in the air makes it difficult to breathe sometimes. That was probably why I wasn't feeling well this morning as I returned to the compound from my daily trek to the grocery store. I was carrying two heavy sacks of groceries and was out of breath from walking up the hill. Plus, I had been in a bad mood for several days after getting rather drunk at El Balcón a few nights ago. So I definitely was not in the mood to listen to Joey when he approached me as I stepped inside the front gate.

He started off with, "Do you know what the two fundamental laws of the universe are?"

"I don't care, Joey," I said.

But he ignored me and continued, "They are that everything organic rots; and everything inorganic erodes."

I just shook my head no and kept walking to my apartment. But he walked along side of me and continued talking.

"Think about it," he said. "Everything organic is in the continual process of putridation."

"That's not even a word, Joey," I snapped.

"Oh... well I meant decaying, decomposing, smelling putrid. Nothing stays the same. It all rots."

We got as far as the steps that go up to the second floor. I didn't want him following me upstairs to my apartment. I stopped and faced him.

"As I said, Joey, I don't care. Even if everything is constantly changing, I don't give a shit. It can all rot away for all I care."

"But don't you see? That violates the first law of thermodynamics—that everything remains constant and never increases or decreases."

I raised my voice a notch. "And I don't care, Joey! It doesn't affect me."

"But it means you're dying!" he retorted. "And I'm dying. We're all dying and it all means nothing."

"Not me," I blurted out. "I'm already dead," and I turned and walked up the stairs. He just stood there at the foot of the staircase watching me.

I shouldn't have yelled at him, but my head was pounding. I used to think of myself as eminently rational, logical, and in control... but I'm not. I'm irrational, impulsive, and totally ruled by whatever my emotions or senses are feeling at the moment. I made a mental note to apologize to him later.

I stepped into my apartment and placed the two bags of groceries on the kitchen counter. I washed my hands, got out the spray bottle of alcohol, and began wiping down each jar or can as I took them out of the bags and put them away—the standard protocol, thanks to coronavirus. It's so ingrained in me now, that I don't even think about it. I remember when I first moved to Panama a decade ago, I had to adjust to washing all fruits and vegetables in vinegar before preparing a meal—the standard protocol for killing parasites in tropical countries. It just becomes a habit you don't even think about. Life is the same way—it becomes a habit you don't even think about.

The ritual of putting the groceries away seemed to calm me down. I didn't know why I was so out of breath walking back from the store. It's only two blocks, but it is a rather steep hill coming back. I thought to myself that maybe it was time for a routine check-up with my cardiologist. I thought again about what a rough year it had been. I counted the months—it had been nine months since my hospitalization in Toledo. Nine months, just enough time for something new to have been born, and yet... what had I done with the time except drink and hang out with other gringos?

I told myself that I have been recuperating, gathering my strength, getting better, preparing myself to travel again, to go back to Europe again, to visit Spain and Toledo again, to pick up life where I left it off.

Joey was right about one thing: everything organic rots. Buddha said it almost three thousand years ago: *I am impermanent and subject to decay; I am impermanent and subject to disease; I am impermanent and subject to death; I will lose all that I love; I will inherit the consequences of my actions.*

I sat down in my one good chair and thought about this. What a waste, all this life, what a waste. It all slipped through my fingers while I was alive, and it just continued to slip through my fingers after I died. That must be the nature of life, like quicksilver, like smoke, it just flows around you, enticing you, seducing you, but never staying with you. It always flows away.

And there's nothing we can do about it. Even after I was given this gift of death and realized how life flows away, did I change a single thing in my life? No! I just continued to drink at El Balcón with my friends, to avoid the people I detested, to structure my time with little daily habits and rituals. I was never involved in life. I did try to help Tom, but I would have done that anyway, and besides, it made no difference. He lost his money and had to go back to the States. Did my words make any difference, or was he fated to do that, the same way I was destined to spend ten years of afternoons in a Panamanian bar?

I don't know if it's possible for a person to change. I only know that I haven't. Even *after* dying, I simply didn't change.

CHAPTER TWENTY-ONE

I must be dreaming. There's that black crow again, diving straight down into the fog. When he hits the fog, he disappears. I think he's gone. But then he reappears from a different portion of the fog, flying straight upwards. My head hurts, but I strain to watch him more. There's that drumming sound—rhythmic, constant... it irritates me, like someone tapping a drumstick constantly. I look for the crow again. There he is, diving into the fog in time to the drumming. He's gone into the gray mist. Wait, there he is, flying upwards. I squint to see. There's something in his beak. It's a tiny fish. Beads of water seem to be flying off the crow. I want to see him clearer, but my eyes are full of crust. I try to move my left hand to rub my eyes, but I can't. It's restrained, held down by something. I pull my right arm free, and rub my eyes, and stare at the crow again. He's sitting on a branch with the fish still in his beak. He tilts his head upward and swallows the fish. He opens his wings and flies up. I blink and squint more. He's not a crow. I can see that now. He's a black heron. There—he's diving down into the fog. But I can tell now it's *not* fog. It's water. Deep running water. He emerges a minute later with another fish impaled on his beak. He flies up to the branch to eat it. I blink and look again.

Suddenly, there's a loud rushing sound and everything snaps into place. There is a horrific pain in my head. My mouth is dry. My face hurts. My whole body hurts.

I look down. I'm lying in a bed. Not my bed. There are metal guardrails up on both sides. I look at my left arm. It is loosely tied to the metal railing with white gauze so I can only move it about twelve inches. There is a needle in my arm, covered with a bandage, and a clear plastic tube running up to a bottle of liquid. I'm on an IV. There are bandages on my chest with wires running over my right side to some machine. I try and turn to look. There are lights and lines moving... and a beeping, steady rhythmically, with an echo sound, but constant like tapping.

I'm in a hospital.

I try and shift my body up on the bed a bit. There is a curtain on the left side of my bed. But the right side of the bed is near a wall. On the wall is a picture, a watercolor of a black heron standing on a log in a pond. I'm in a hospital, a fucking hospital.

I hear voices. The curtain parts. A woman in a white coat carrying a clipboard appears.

"Ah, estas despierto. ¿Hablas español?" she asks.

"Yes," I answer in Spanish. "I speak Spanish. Where am I?"

She doesn't answer me but glances at some papers in a file on her clipboard, then looks at me and asks, "How are you feeling?"

"Confused," I said. "Where am I? Who are you?"

"I'm Doctor Cristina Martin. This is the Cervantes Hospital in Toledo. You walked into our emergency room yesterday. Do you remember that?"

"Yesterday? I did that yesterday?"

"Yes. Your heart was in fibrillation. It was very dangerous. You told us you had been suffering from this for a week before you came in."

"I did?"

She looked at the file on her clipboard. "Yes. You were lucky you came in when you did. We almost lost you last night."

She looked directly at me. I noticed that she had beautiful brown eyes.

"This is Toledo, Spain?" I asked.

She smiled. "Yes. You're in Toledo, Spain. We had to give you a mild sedative last night to keep you from thrashing around. So, you're probably still a little groggy. I will have them bring you some breakfast. We will talk after you've had something to eat."

With that she turned and walked away. Through the parted curtain I could see her talking to some nurses at a nurses' station.

I looked around again. I could focus my eyes this time. This was clearly a hospital bed. I was in a hospital gown. There were what I assumed were electrodes taped to my chest with wires running over to a machine next to the bed. If I turned my head far enough up and to the right, I could see the moving line tracing my heartbeat on a small screen. The machine was making a rhythmic beep/clicking sound. That must have been the sound I was hearing while I was watching that crow dive into the fog. I looked again at the picture on the wall. It was just a print of a watercolor of a black heron standing on a log over some water. Each time I blinked, things were more in focus. My senses seemed to be waking up. I became aware of how uncomfortable the bed was. All the muscles in my back hurt. I felt something draped over my leg. I lifted up the sheet and saw a tube running out from under my gown and over my right knee. I reached my right arm down and discovered that I had a catheter in me. Well, *this* is a first, I thought. I've never had that before. I lay my head back on the pillow. I looked over at the IV in my left arm held in place by adhesive tape. There was a loop of gauze around my arm that was loosely tied to the left metal bed railing. That rope of gauze was obviously meant to keep me from turning over onto my right side or face down to sleep, to keep from dislodging the IV or the electrodes. That meant I must have slept—if you could call it sleep—on my back all night. No wonder my back hurt.

A nurse came in and, without saying a word, raised the back of my bed up so I was almost in a sitting position. A minute later another nurse brought in a table on wheels. She untied the rope of gauze that was around my left arm, lowered the left guardrail, and rolled the table over my lap up to my chest. On the table was orange juice, some pieces of bread, and a small bowl of fruit. Not much of a breakfast, I thought. Still I was glad to have anything. But what I really wanted was coffee.

"¿Es posible tomar un café?" I asked.

"No señor, no hay café para usted," she said. No coffee for me.

I ate everything they brought. Food seemed to turn on some logical part of my brain, although it was not working at full capacity. The last thing I remembered was talking to Joey. That couldn't have been a dream. None of what I lived through for the past nine months could have been a dream—it was all too real. I must have come back to Toledo, but I didn't remember that. Did I live through the rainy season and then fly back to Spain? Did I have some kind of stroke and simply did not remember coming back to Toledo? I wiggled my toes on my left and right feet. I wiggled my fingers on both hands. I moved my mouth around. There was no sign of paralysis or weak muscle. How did I get back here?

The nurse came and took the table and empty food tray away. I would have killed for a cup of coffee. Coffee always helps me think. I lay there and tried to force myself to think. The doctor said that they gave me a sedative last night. That might explain why I couldn't remember coming back to Toledo or coming to this hospital again. Again? Was this the same hospital? Did I come back to the same hospital, or was this a *different* hospital? The more I thought about it, the more it was apparent that I must have left Villa Rosario sometime during the rainy season and come back to Spain. There was no other explanation, because otherwise I would not remember having the fibrillation in Toledo and leaving Toledo and flying back to Villa Rosario.

Once I decided that that had to be the case, I relaxed a bit. Obviously, when the effects of the sedative wore off, all my memory would come back to me, and I would remember everything leading up to this moment: the decision to return to Toledo, the packing, the saying goodbye to Emile, Ralph, Dave, and even Joey. All I had to do was wait for the sedative to wear off. Then I would remember flying out of Panama. Did I fly to Lisbon and travel around Portugal for a few weeks like I did last year and then continue on to Madrid and Toledo? Or did I fly directly from Panama to Madrid and take the train south to Toledo? I simply couldn't remember. But I knew it would come back to me. The other reason I knew that all my memories of the last nine months were real was because the details didn't fade the longer I was awake. A dream, even a vivid dream, evaporates quickly after one awakens. But all the details of my conversations with Emile, my feelings about Herald, my vlogs for the *Solipsistic Times*... all of those things remained exactly the same as each minute went by. Those were *real* memories. I knew this because they *felt real*. They had the quality of real experience; they were internally consistent, sequential, and logical. They didn't evaporate.

I lay there and thought about things. I must have had another fibrillation attack. That was the obvious explanation. I had had the first one nine months ago; had returned to Villa Rosario to recuperate; obviously hadn't recuperated long enough; and had decided to come back to Toledo to finish the vacation that got interrupted last year. That would be just like me, I told myself—to impulsively rush back into active traveling before my body was ready. I bet I didn't even consult my cardiologist. Well, this was my reward then. I overdid it again, and my body shut me down. I told myself I had to face the fact that I was getting older and simply couldn't travel the way I used to. I hoped I didn't do any damage to my heart this time. I seemed to feel okay. Then I wondered about my hotel room. I didn't recall checking out. Were all my things still there? Did I stay at the same hotel as I did last year? I wondered for how long I'd booked it for. I couldn't remember. I couldn't even remember what day or month it was.

Then I realized that it was pointless to try and figure anything out or make plans until after the sedative wore completely off. Obviously, I was not thinking with a completely full deck. I took a deep breath and told myself to be patient.

A different nurse came in holding a clipboard. She did not look at me, but rather walked over to the machine and wrote down something in the file on the clipboard. I figured that she must just be a charting nurse

She turned to leave, but I spoke up. "Excuse me," I said in Spanish. "Can you tell me the date?"

She looked a bit startled. "La fecha?" she asked.

"Yes, please," I said, "the date, you know, day, month, year..."

She thought for a second and then told me, and then walked away.

My stomach dropped. This was nine months ago! I had never left Toledo! I was *back in time* in Toledo! This was the first hospitalization, nine months ago! This was not possible! This must be a dream. I reached over with my right hand and grabbed my left wrist and squeezed it hard. My brain began to race. I felt like I might throw up. I made myself take a slow breath and looked around again. This did not feel like a dream. This felt like reality. Was it possible that everything that happened in Villa Rosario after I had left Toledo was *all* a dream? I tried to pick one memory and think about it. I remembered sitting in El Balcón talking to Tom, telling him not to trust Herald. I remember my argument exactly, how it was illogical that Herald would not have invested in bitcoins if his cousin was such a bitcoin genius. And I remember pointing out the two hookers at the bar to Tom and pointing out that Herald was so cheap he wouldn't spring for them. And I remember Tom agreeing with me as we sat there at the back table that we gringos always sat at. That didn't happen *before* I came to Toledo! That happened *after* I had the fibrillation attack in Toledo and returned home to Villa Rosario to recuperate. That memory was crystal clear to me. This made no sense! One of these two experiences had to be a dream.

I closed my eyes, and once again, tried to control my breathing. I told myself to take things slowly, to remember that they had given me some type of drug last night. I did the only thing I know how to do when panic hits: to just focus on the here and now moment, to just breathe in and out, and just be in the moment, to not figure out the past or jump to the future. Just breathe, I told myself. You're in a hospital bed... actually, you're confined to the hospital bed by tubes and wires. You can't go anywhere quite yet. Just be here, and let these events unfold and see what happens. I closed my eyes. Maybe I should try and force myself to sleep, I thought.

I think I did actually drift into a light sleep, but then I heard someone walk up to the bed. I opened my eyes. It was Dr. Martin again. She was still holding a clipboard with what I assumed was my chart on it. The left guardrail of the bed was still in the down position, and she sat down on the edge of the bed and looked at me.

"Are you feeling better?" she asked.

"Yes and no," I said. "I still feel confused. I'm... I'm trying to make sense out of what happened."

"You were thrashing around last night, so we gave you a mild sedative. We didn't want you to tear the IV out of your arm. The grogginess will wear off soon."

She glanced up at the EKG machine. "Were you on vacation in Toledo?" she asked.

"Yes."

"From the United States?"

"Well, from Panama. I live in Panama, but I'm from the States originally."

"How long is your vacation? When were you planning to go home?"

Her questions seemed to awaken the memory of how I got to Toledo. "I left Panama about a month ago," I said. "It's the rainy season there. I always come to Europe during Panama's rainy season. I was just traveling around. I like to travel. I arrived in Madrid last week from Portugal. I've been in Toledo for about a week. I'm supposed to go to Zurich in a few days. I have a plane ticket back to Panama in another two weeks or so."

"Your heart was in fibrillation for several days," she said. "We gave you a lot of medicine last night to bring it back into a normal rhythm. I'm going to give you several prescriptions, and we are going to discharge you this morning. There's a pharmacy on the first floor. Do you have a regular cardiologist back in Panama?"

I nodded my head yes.

"You could, of course, continue with your vacation if you take it easy. But if your heart goes back into fibrillation, you will need to get to an emergency room right away. It's up to you, but I think the better plan would be to go back home, to see your regular cardiologist. It's up to you, but I think it would be wiser to cut your vacation short."

I nodded my head yes again. "Yes, yes, I will do that."

"I will prepare a report you can take to your doctor," she said. She flipped through the pages in the chart. "You told us yesterday you take Atenolol, Ibersartin, and aspirin every day?"

"Yes."

"I'm going to change those medications. Your doctor may change them back, but until you see your doctor, take the new prescriptions."

"Okay," I said.

"One of the prescriptions I'm going to give you is an anticoagulant. So, no more aspirin for you, understand?"

"Yes."

"And no more coffee... and you told us you drink. I'm sorry, but no more alcohol."

"No coffee and no alcohol?"

"No coffee, no alcohol. This was pretty serious. You need to let your heart get better."

I nodded okay. I must have looked forlorn, because she smiled and said, "Be happy, you're still alive. You're going to be okay."

With that, she stood up and said, "We'll probably discharge you in a few hours. We just want to see that you're stable. So just relax for a while." And she walked out between the curtains.

I lay there for a few minutes, really unable to absorb it all. This clearly was real—it felt real. Events were moving sequentially; time had a regularity to it; my body aches felt real. The tube in my arm and the wires on my chest felt real enough. But my memory of the last nine months in Villa Rosario felt equally as real. I couldn't reconcile the two, and I couldn't hold them in my head at the same time—it made me feel too anxious, almost crazy, to think of them both as real. So, in order to maintain my sanity, I had to assume that the memories of Villa Rosario were false, that they were only so vivid because of whatever sedative they had given me last night. I would know soon enough, I realized. If the memories were false, Tom would still be at the apartment complex. There would be no new fonda next to the Chinese hardware store. The *Solipsistic Times* would not have the nine months' worth of vlogs that I had written in their archives. Herald would not have been murdered—well actually, I realized, Herald would not even exist because he arrived after I had returned from Toledo. He was not a real person—he was just someone I conjured up. Good, I thought. I can purge the memory of that ugly American. What a creation he had been. He must have oozed up from the deepest darkest part of my soul. I began to feel more secure. I closed my eyes and actually drifted back to sleep for a few minutes. When I awoke, I was still in the hospital bed. This was real.

CHAPTER TWENTY-TWO

As the effects of the sedative wore off, I became more aware of how much my body ached from being in the same prone position all night. I calculated that I had been in that bed for almost twenty hours. So I was very glad when the nurses came in to remove the IV, the catheter, and all the electrodes. They brought me my clothes, helped me to stand up from the bed, and then closed the curtains as they left, so that I could dress myself. I was a little unsteady on my feet, but happy to be standing and moving. I noticed that it was easier to breathe. While I felt weak, I didn't feel tired or dizzy. Whatever medicine they gave me in the IV all night must have worked miracles on my heart. I was glad to be alive. Colors seemed brighter, more immediate. Also, I noticed that my brain seemed to be reformatting the last nine months of memories of Villa Rosario and moving them to the "dream" category. I could still recall all the details, but I had to make an effort to do so. It was as if my brain was moving them all off the front burner of my awareness and onto the back burners— still reachable, but not as important. I was glad about this. In fact, I think I was willing my brain to do this—if that's possible—because it was just too disconcerting, almost nauseating, to think about the two realities. I felt real being in Toledo, even if it all had a slight déjà vu feeling to it.

I talked again with the doctor. She gave me a handful of prescriptions and a four-page medical summary for my cardiologist in Panama. I thanked her profusely. A nurse walked me downstairs to the pharmacy where I filled the prescriptions. The nurse told me that there was a taxi stand just outside the front door of the hospital. I went outside into the bright sunlight, got into a taxi, told them the name of my hotel, and away we went.

I recognized the hotel as soon as the taxi approached it. It was the same one that I remembered staying in... well, staying in. I almost started to frame the thought as "staying in *before*"... but this was before, or rather, this was now, and my brain automatically reframed the feeling as me simply recognizing—with a rather warm friendly feeling—the hotel.

The desk clerk nodded at me as I walked by. I went up to my room and took a hot shower. That felt great. I put on fresh clothes and then was ready to face a number of tasks.

But first I had to eat. The meagre breakfast they gave me at the hospital had long worn off, and I was famished. I knew there was a small outdoor café one block from the hotel so I went there. I knew I had eaten there a few days ago, but I couldn't remember if I had eaten there after I had gotten released from the hospital before, but in any case, I was going to eat there today. I picked a table with an umbrella to block the sun and ordered a sautéed salmon, salad, and potatoes. I would have normally had a glass of wine with lunch, but I had some herbal tea instead.

After lunch I went back to the hotel. Now I had the strength to do what needed to be done, which was to cancel my upcoming flight from Madrid to Zurich, cancel my hotel in Zurich, cancel my plane from Zurich to Panama, and book a new flight as soon as possible from Madrid back to Panama. I knew I was going to lose a ton of money on this, but I wasn't going to take chances with my health.

Money can't help you when you're dead...

When that thought crossed my mind, I had a sudden epiphany! Since I was *back* in Toledo, that meant I hadn't died! I know that sounds obvious, but the implications were profound. If I wasn't dead, I could have new experiences again! I wouldn't have to recycle old memories. Life wouldn't be a dream; it would be real and unpredictable. It didn't have to be stale anymore. When I realized this, I started to feel excited. In fact, I hadn't been this excited, this hopeful, during the entire nine months when I was dead. I would be able to do new things! First, of course, I had to get back to Villa Rosario and see my cardiologist and recuperate.

I knew from experience that the Wi-Fi in my hotel room was not the best, so I took my laptop and my cellphone and went down to the hotel lobby where the Wi-Fi was strong. I had the lobby all to myself. I took a seat on the large leather couch and called the hotel in Zurich first and cancelled my room, explaining that I had a health issue and had to return home. They were gracious and refunded my deposit. Then I cancelled the flight from Madrid to Zurich. They were not gracious and refused to refund my ticket, but it was only eighty euros. Then I cancelled the flight from Zurich to Panama that was supposed to occur in two and a half weeks. I got a partial refund on that. Then I opened my laptop and looked for flights from Madrid back to Panama. I found one for the next day at noon. It was a direct flight of eleven hours, but with the time difference, that meant I would arrive in Panama in the late afternoon of technically the same day. That would work. I booked it. More money spent, but I didn't care. I was buying my future. I would just spend another night at this hotel and then take the morning train from Toledo to the Madrid railway station, and then a shuttle bus to the Madrid airport.

The only thing left was to arrange a ride from Panama City back to Villa Rosario. It's possible to take a bus from the Panama airport to La Chorrera, and then catch another bus to Villa Rosario, but after an eleven-hour plane ride I knew I would be in no mood for buses. I looked at the time. It would be evening in Panama now, but not too late to call Emile. I dialed his number. I decided not to tell him about my fibrillation episode.

"Hello Emile," I said, "I hope I'm not calling too late."

"No, no, not at all. How are you? How's Europe?"

"Europe is wonderful, but I've decided to come home a bit early, and I have a favor to ask. I booked a flight that arrives at the Tocumen airport at four p.m. tomorrow. Would it be possible for you to pick me up there?"

"Tomorrow at four? Let me check my calendar… tomorrow, tomorrow… oh, it looks like I'm free all day! Ha, in fact, I'm free all this week. Of course, my friend, I will be there. What airline?"

"Iberia."

"Okay, let's see… Your plane lands at four. You'll need thirty minutes to get through immigration and customs… I'll park in the passenger pick-up lot. You text me when you're through with customs, and I'll pull up to the usual pick-up lane."

"That would be great, Emile. I owe you. How's everything in Panama?"

"Wet, rainy. Ha, are you sure you want to come back?"

"Yeah. Everyone doing okay there?"

"It's pretty much the same. We lost power most of yesterday, but it's back on now. Joey's on some kick about the World Bank and the Illuminati. Ralph's got a crush on some hooker who works at El Balcón. Dave's doing alright. Tom's outdrinking all of us."

"Ha, sounds about normal."

"The landlord told me we got some new guy moving in next week, in the vacant apartment next to Ralph."

"Oh?" I said.

"Yes, another gringo. I think his name is Herald."

My stomach dropped. There was a sudden rushing in my ears.

"Is he from Oklahoma?" I managed to ask.

"Yes, I think he is. Do you know him?"

"No," I said.

There was a pause in the conversation.

"It was just a wild guess," I added.

"Well, okay then, I'll see you tomorrow around four-thirty."

"Yes… yes, thanks again Emile. See you then."

I hung up and just sat there on the lobby sofa.

"Well, fuck me," I said out loud to no one.

—FIN—

ABOUT THE AUTHOR

Robert Rahula was born in Spain to an American father and Spanish mother, but grew up in Virginia on the farm of his paternal grandparents. He returned to Menorca, Spain, in the 1960s to pursue his writing career. Over the past forty years, Robert has published dozens of books of prose and poetry in Spain and in the United States. Readings of his poems appear on his YouTube channel, his Facebook page, and his website robertrahula.com. He travels Europe, Central and South America for several months a year, giving readings and lectures, and spends the rest of his time writing.